ALGOMA'S REVENGE

(BALAVAN BOOK THREE)

SYLVIA S. LEE

MEGAN H. LEE

Prologue

Peace is a wonderful thing. It would be hard to find anyone in the world who would argue with that, but what is peace, really? Is it just the lack of turmoil or something much deeper than that? After the Six Year War ended, Balavan was indeed at a state of peace and tranquility. The end of all of that fighting means no more bloodshed. Tears are now coming from joy rather than sadness. Screams are now from merriment rather than terror. While most people agree that this is the perfect definition of peace, Trip is not one of them.

Despite the tranquility on the streets, not everyone feels at peace. Ironically, Trip feels more unease now than any time during the war. In battle, his nerves of steel have earned him the moniker El Diablo. By not fearing death, being shot at by the enemy is just another day at the office to him. In peace, what does the devil do? Sitting in his posh office is like torture to him. While visiting his garden does give him a sense of serenity, the feeling is sort lived. He knows that there are other things he should be doing that can make a difference in the world. While Thom is immersed in his own battles for redemption, Trip is on his own mission to find peace within himself.

Chapter 1: Bitter Memories

Pacing back and forth, Trip is getting restless. While he is glad that he has avenged his family by catching the villain who destroyed his village, he knows there is more he needs to do – he needs to get back to his roots. As Violet can attest, he does not like to be a leader. He only did it so he can capture Victor. If he has a choice, he much prefers to be back in the desert with nothing more than his garden under a clear blue sky hunting and gathering only what he needs for survival rather than sitting in a stuffy office discussing politics day in and day out.

Who can blame him? He has never been much of a talker. He much prefers to do something about what is bothering him than to talk about it.

Violet can tell that he has something in his mind and is itching to get to it. He seems to be getting deeper and deeper in thought with each passing day. On a particularly dark and gloomy evening, his mood seems to match the atmosphere, but, as usual, he has no intention of divulging any of his private thoughts without a little encouragement. While everyone else is chattering amongst themselves intermingled with bouts of laughter at the table, he is simply playing with his usual bottle of potent concoction that he calls food.

"So, how do you like your dinner?" she starts with a little small talk.

Knowing that she can care less what the answer to that question is, Trip replies with a casual, "It's cool."

After knowing him for so long, she knows what it really means. That is code for: *I really don't care. Please just leave me alone.*

"So, what's next?" she continues, pretending not to get the message.

By dishing out a very open ended question like this, Violet is hoping that he will steer the conversation where *she* wants him to without looking like it. Of course, Trip knows his best friend too well not to see through that line of questioning.

"Why don't you come out and ask what you want to ask?" Trip says without taking his eyes off of the table.

"OK, you asked for it!" Violet says excitedly as she puts her arm around his neck. "Are you going to leave me soon?" she asks with puppy eyes.

"Oh, come on. That's hardly fair. You know I can never *leave* you," Trip says with a slight hint of sarcasm.

"OK, fine, Mr. Technicality. Are you going to leave our *headquarters* physically anytime soon?"

Turning into a more serious look, he admits, "Yes."

Despite knowing that would be his answer, she is a little disappointed for him to confirm it.

Not to sound like a naysayer, she replies, "I understand. I hope you accomplish whatever it is you set out to achieve. Do you need any help?" Violet asks knowing exactly what the answer is.

As expected, she gets a simple "Thanks, but I am good" before taking off.

Rolling her eyes, Violet instantly knows that she had asked the wrong question. Trip never *needs* any help. Ever since he recovered from that fateful day when Victor destroyed his life, he has not *needed* any assistance from anyone. That is not to say that he doesn't make a mistake or welcome a hand once in a while. It's just that he knows how to recover from it by himself. She should have asked a question that doesn't insinuate that he cannot take care of

2

himself like whether or not he would like to have company or something along those lines.

Nevertheless, she is still annoyed that he has to be so distant all the time. Whenever he feels that she is going to be on one of her long winded discussions, he always gets up and leaves the first chance he gets. It's getting old. It's not like he has anything to hide. Besides, they know *everything* about each other from their favorite hiding places to their worst fears, but everything she knows about him is gathered throughout many years and mostly by chance.

On the other hand, she has no problem telling him anything he wants to know, but he never asks. That does not stop her from sharing when they are in private. The truth of the matter is, he *does* want to know, because he does care about her, but he does not want to sound intrusive, even though she is the one offering the information. Now, she is hoping that their friendship is strong enough for him to include her on his newest venture, but she knows better.

Racing after him, she realizes that there is no point. He has already disappeared from view. Instead, she heads straight for his garden. At a time like this, that would be the only place he would go. Within a minute, he shows up like clockwork.

"Surprised to see me?" Violet asks teasingly.

"You know I am not."

"OK, I am just going to ask right out. Where are you going?"

"I don't know."

She knows that he has a good idea where he wants to go. She also knows that his answer is not a deliberate attempt at brushing her off. Instead, he is answering truthfully, but not to the question that she means to ask. Yes, that sounds confusing, but that is just another thing about Trip. He can be *so* literal sometimes. If she asks him to watch the pot, he would literally just look at it. Like a child, he would even let it bubble over into a giant mess, but would not do anything about it. In this case, it seems he does not know the exact physical location that he wants to go, but he has an idea of something. He just hasn't been able to put his finger on it yet. After thinking for a second, she rephrases her question.

"OK, what are you looking for?"

Now, that is a question that Trip can answer. "My past," he answers without looking up from the beautiful purple rose.

Ah, she is glad that she asked the right question this time. Even though she still cannot get his full attention, at least he answered with a useful response. Looking at the rose, she can see why he cannot take his eyes off of it. It seems the flowers are even prettier now that the war is over. Perhaps, there is a logical reason. The skies are definitely clearer without the smokes coming out of the heavy artilleries. Without the soot in the air or the blood flowing into the rivers and contaminating the water source, every flower in the garden is blooming ever so beautifully. They even smell sweeter as they invite hundreds of insects to dance around the petals.

"How do you plan on finding it?" Violet says, knowing this is a difficult question to ask, considering that his home was burned to the ground.

Like the previous questions, they can be a little rhetorical. Since they have never returned to the original location, neither of them knows whether or not there is anything left of Algoma, the Land of the Desert. Because Violet's tribesmen are nomads who move all year round, it's difficult to find anyone who could pinpoint the exact location. The only thing they really have is a general direction and an approximate number of days that it took to

4

get to Balavan since they rescued Trip that day. With so much time passed, even Violet cannot remember much. Of course, since Trip himself was quite delusional and was passed out for parts of the time, he cannot possibly remember anything useful either.

It's not like they have any other way of locating it. Ever since that fateful day, no one has heard about it or from it. There has not been a single person claiming to be from there entering Balavan over the years. To outsiders, it's like the entire land just vanished into thin air. Yet, Trip is convinced that there must have been some survivors left, somewhere. He cannot possibly be the only one who escaped the slaughter. They may have staggered to nearby towns, but there has to be some. It may just be wishful thinking, but perhaps, when the dust settled, they may have even returned to rebuild it. At least that is what he is hoping for.

He can no longer stay in Balavan standing idly by. He has to find out and see if there is any way he can reconnect with his people or help his hometown become its former self again. Even though he is as much a Balavian as the next man now, he knows that a part of him will always be an Algomian no matter how many years it has been since he last saw it. As long as he heads for the right direction, he is confident that he will find it.

"You know where," Trip finally says after pausing for a second.

"When are you leaving?"

"In the morning."

"I guess there is no point asking whether or not you want company."

"You know the answer to that, too."

"Yes." Violet says. "Why does he have to be such a hard head all the time," she says to herself angrily.

Even though her mind tells her that he can take care of himself, her heart tells her otherwise. While he is undeniably the toughest man she has ever know, he is not indestructible, despite what his reputation may suggest. With his current set of mind, he may not be as sharp as he usually is. All it takes is one small mistake and he can be in deep trouble. If he goes at it alone, who is going to be there to watch his back? She cannot possibly face it if something were to happen to him.

Yet, Violet knows that she cannot possibly go with him. If she does, it would leave the Desiderios without an official leader. Even if she appoints someone to take her place, she knows the former members of the Legionnaires will take the opportunity to start up an insurgence again. Because it has been a while since her subordinates have seen peace, many of them are taking advantage of the new, calmer regime and beginning to get lazy. There are others who are becoming agitated. Ironically, the best soldiers during war time are also the worst ones during peaceful ones because they live on the excitement of the danger and the uncertainty. Someone has to keep them in line before something goes wrong.

Then again, she really wants to go with him. For as long as she can remember, he has been by her side, one way or another. It will definitely be hard to let him go. The only consolation is that she knows he will miss her, too, even if he will not admit it. Instead of her usual enthusiastic hug, she slowly walks up to him and pats his back while she avoids eye contact with him. She is not going to say good-bye because it will be too difficult for him.

She also knows that he will leave before anyone else awakens in the morning to avoid having to say his farewell to her, too. There is no point asking him when he will be back because she already knows that he has no clue, but she knows he will come back for her. That doesn't mean she will stop worrying about him every single day until his return.

*

At 4AM, Trip is up and ready for his journey. Meanwhile, Violet has not slept. She cannot possibly sleep knowing that she will not see him again for a long time. Tossing and turning, all she can think of are the times that they have had together.

While not all of it has been good, in fact, a great deal of it is not, she would not trade a moment of it for anything in the world. Looking down at her arm, she sees quite a few battle wounds, which makes her smile. Every scar reminds her of a different mêlée she has been in with him. It's quite bitter sweet.

From her room, she can usually hear his door open. In the dead of the night, it is louder than normal. If she concentrates a little, she can almost hear him get out of bed and walk to his closet to change despite his propensity to be stealthy. Although she does not want him to see her, she cannot help but follow his every move until he leaves.

Sensing that he is leaving, she quickly puts on an all-black outfit. While she absolutely hates such a gloomy getup, it is a tribute to Trip as well as a disguise. After all, if she goes around dressed in her bright dress, it will be that much harder for her to tail him without being noticed. But, it's all for nothing. As soon as she opens the door, he turns around, looks her straight in the eyes with a smile and says, "Don't be a stranger."

Smiling, she opens her mouth to say something witty, but decides not to. It's no use. He will not be able to hear it anyways. Before she can utter a word, he is already gone. As she walks sadly back to her room, she sees a package on her bed. She knows instantly who it's from. The question is – how and when did he put it there? Impressed, but hardly surprised, she knows that he is the best and this proves it. As she opens the box, it's a plain book with – what else – a black cover. Although there are no names or drawing to indicate who it came from, she already knows that it's from her best friend.

As she opens up the first page, it simply has a giant "XO" across the page in red ink. As tears flows from her eyes, she continues to flip through the pages, careful not to stain it. Each page has carefully pressed dry flowers from the garden that he loves with nothing else. There are no captions, because none is needed. This is definitely one of those moments in life where less is more. Holding the book close to her heart, she knows this will be her most treasured possession for the rest of her life.

She regrets not given him a memento to remember her by, but she knows that Trip is not one to need material things, even if it's for memories. It will only slow him down or get someone in trouble. That is also the reason why he doesn't write anything down. As far as he is concerned, anyone can use tangible evidence against him by learning about loved ones or even friends and using them as leverage.

Or, they can find out about his plans by analyzing the writings. No, thanks. Besides, he never forgets anything important even if he doesn't mention it for years. He will always remember every detail of her face as long as he is alive.

*

Leaving everything with Violet, he is confident that Balavan is in good hands. There is absolutely no need to worry because he trusts that she can overcome any obstacle, not matter how difficult. He would not wake up screaming in fear that she is dead or that Balavan has been burned to the ground, because he has complete and total faith in her. Hence, there is nothing stopping him from looking forward. He has a long journey ahead of him if he wants to find out what happened to his childhood home over those years. Although he has never discussed it, it is obvious that it still leaves a giant scar on him. There are still days when he would wake up from a nightmare pouring in sweat. It's the only thing that he has every feared in his life.

In it, he would see a black ghostly figure with piercing blue eyes charging at him on a demon horse that snorts fire. Every time, he would be standing there in his nightmare, not knowing what to do. Even if he tried to fight, nothing ever hits the enemy. He can try to pick up rocks to throw at them, but they would turn into sand that disappears in the wind. He can shoot an arrow, but it would always land short of the target. He can lounge and charge at them, but he would never seem to be able to reach them.

It's obvious that capturing Victor is not enough. He has to do more. Even if there is nothing he can do, he wants to know for sure. He needs to return to Algoma and see it with his own eyes. . Even though it has been 23 years, he remembers everything in great detail both before and after the massacre, as if it were all only yesterday. He vividly remembers the sheer serenity and beauty of it all before it was destroyed so utterly and totally.

Most of all, he remembers his parents. Like most other people in the village, they were farmers who tended various crops and kept many types of animals. It was backbreaking work, but they always did it every day with a smile on their faces because they always knew that they were doing an honest day's work. They didn't have much, but whatever they had, they would give to him.

Being an only child, he had their full attention. No matter what it was that they were doing, they were always there for him when he needed them, no matter how trivial. If he scrapped his knee, his mother was always there to clean and nurse it. If he needed advice, his father was always there to listen before giving his honest opinion. They never punished him, not because he was spoiled, but because he never gave them a reason to. In fact, it was quite the opposite. His parents wanted to give him things, but he always refused them.

When every other child in the land wanted a new toy and would do nothing more than talk about it until they got one, he could care less about it. Instead, he always preferred the open air. The fresh smell of a morning bloom trumps any new gadget any day. When he was indoors, he always enjoyed the company of his doting parents the best, especially his mother's smile that could turn any bad day into a sunny one and his father's humor that could make him cry in joy. In a way, they remind him of Violet.

"Come on, get a hold of yourself" he tells himself, "not every fond memory leads back to her."

Then, he remembers their charred bodies. He could hardly recognize them, but he did. They were fighting next to each other and were cut down in their prime. They were only a foot away from one another. He was not there when they were killed. While a part of him is mad that he was not by their side at the end, another part of him knows that he would not have lived to avenge their deaths if he was. Witnessing their deaths would have completely paralyzed him. With Victor's men on the rampage, they would have certainly taken him out in the process.

When Victor's men finally left, he sat by their bodies for hours as he wished he was dead, too. He wanted them to take him with them. After he finally ran out of tears, he knew he had to bury them, but he had nothing on him, least of all a shovel. With his little hands, he managed to dig a very shallow grave for both of them. He was also too small and weak to carry their bodies. He had to push their bodies in. Even though it may seem crude, it was the best that a small, starving, and injured boy could do at the time. At least, they had each other in the afterlife.

After putting the dirt over them, he was hoping that it was enough to prevent the hyenas and other scavengers from digging them up. It probably was. With so many dead on that day, animals probably went after those who were not buried for their meals and left his parents alone. If he could have, he would have buried them all, but it was an impossible task for a boy so young.

Uh, the more he thinks about it, the more he wants to go back and strangle Victor with his bare hands, but he knows he cannot do that. At his old age, what good would come by spilling his blood now? It would only give him a momentary sense of satisfaction that would quickly pass. It doesn't mean anything anyways. It would not get his childhood back. It would certainly not get him his parents back.

Instead, he tries to focus on happier times by remembering his childhood friends, but he cannot think of many. He does remember a girl who is a couple of years older than him. Once again, she reminds him of Violet, not the same way that his parents remind him of her, of course. They used to hang out in the desert together all the time. They were almost inseparable. It's odd that he hasn't thought about her until today.

One thing they loved to do was to race against one another to see who would win. Unfortunately for him, she

11

always did – every single time. It used to upset him that he could never beat her. Like an older sister, she would always tease him for losing, too. Even though she was never mean-spirited, it would always sting. Now, it is such a distant memory.

For the life of him, he cannot recall her name. Apparently, the name is not nearly as important as the person. All he can think of is that she was quite pretty, but not in a beauty queen way, but in a delicate and mysterious way. It's probably because she always preferred to dress like a tomboy rather than the pink or purple outfits that other girls her age used to way. Nevertheless, he can still see her face clearly. He distinctly remembers that she had freckles, which went with her wavy red hair and joyous green eyes. She was very slender and a little taller than he was. She also used to wear a necklace with a golden snapdragon on it. He hopes she is still alive and that he can meet her again someday.

Besides her, he cannot remember anyone else he could call a friend. Even though he does remember playing with a few of the boys in the area, he cannot say that he remembers any of them. He vaguely remembers that a couple of them have brown hair, but that can be anybody. Guess he really hasn't changed that much. Even though he is surrounded by elite members of the Desiderios, he really only counts Violet as his only true friend. Everyone else is just a fuzz to him.

Chapter 2: Trip's Homecoming

After traveling for a few days, he finally reaches a place that looks familiar. There is nothing specific. It's just a gut feeling. As he looks around, he feels sick to his stomach. He is definitely very close. All of the nightmares that he endured as a child seem to be flooding back into his head. True to his demonic title, however, El Diablo is not about to let anything get in his way.

He continues to walk calmly forward. He immediately recognizes the location where Violet and her family rescued him decades ago. It's nothing more than a big patch of cacti, but he distinctively remembers falling down by it. Back then, it was a much smaller patch, but he is certain that is the location. He remembers the hot sun that was baking his face as he touches his cheeks. It was so different then. Even though he was only a child, everything about his looks said otherwise.

With nothing to eat or drink for days, his face was rough, sunken, and blistered under his filthy, thick, black, and matted hair. His nails were long but split and cracked in so many ways with clumps of dirt and blood underneath them. His clothes were completely torn, showing the infectious open wounds on his body. Parts of his body smelled rancid, not merely from not having bathed for weeks, but from the rotting of his flesh. Violet's family could not have arrived a moment too soon. If he had been in that state even one more day, he would have perished and become vulture food.

As he continued to walk, he sees familiar places that bring back bitter memories. For example, he recalls the spot where he took off his shoes. Because they were barely holding together with holes in the bottom and on the toe areas, he was having trouble walking in them. As soon as he stepped on the burning sand, however, he knew it was a mistake before putting them back on. Although his entire body was numb, the scorching sun turned the sand into an instant frying pan. Without the shoes, he would have cooked the bottom of his feet.

He also sees the site where he almost gave up his will to live. A few days after he left his home town, he was simply wandering in the dessert with nothing but wavy hot sand in front of him. Every direction he looked, it was the same view. There was not a living soul on the horizon, except for the occasional lizard and buzzards flying high above. There might have been some rattlesnakes lurking around, but he was already too delirious to care. Occasionally, he would see an oasis, but would soon realize that it was nothing but a cruel mirage. After several such sightings, he no longer cared for it. After lying down that night, he thought he was never going to wake back up. What did he have to live for? As far as he was concerned, the answer was nothing.

It seems it was not his time. That night, he dreamed of a serene white place surrounded by white flowers and soft fluffy ground, much like clouds.

Then, a little angel came up to him, gave him a big hug, and said, "She is coming to help you soon. Please don't give up yet. If you do, she will be lost, too."

Then, he woke up in the middle of the night. Even though he has no idea who the angel was talking about, he gave him a renewed hope and sense of purpose. Although he was still as lost as before, he knew that if he kept going, he would get out of this alive soon. He just cannot give up. Feeling the cool breeze, he was instantly energized and began to walk again. That was the day that he realized that he needed to walk during the night time to avoid the scorching heat. Perhaps, that was the reason that he managed to stay alive for so long.

*

After traveling for a few more days, he sees the outskirts of a town that looks like where Algoma should have been. Initially, he is a little bewildered. He cannot believe that he has arrived already. Can *this* possibly be his home town? As he recalls, it had taken him *weeks* before being rescued, not mere days. How can this be the place? Then, he realizes what must have happened. Back then, he was tired and delirious. He must have walked in circles a few times without knowing it. Hallucinations can do that to anyone, especially a child.

It was a very different journey than the one he is taking right now. In those days, he was injured, hungry, devastated, and almost gave up on life. Today, he is a much bigger and healthier man, walking at a much faster pace, a clear head, and a determined purpose in mind. Taking a deep breath, he quickens his pace. As he gets closer, he is really surprised at how beautiful it looks.

The lovely desert plants are everywhere. Even from a distance, he recognizes the types of structures on that land. Unlike Balavan where there are large tall buildings, these are small and colorful, just the way he remembers them. He has never seen houses like this anywhere else. In other words, these *must* be Algomians and not another group of people who happened to find a deserted part of land and settled there after the war! With this revelation, he is getting excited. There must have been more survivors than he thought.

As he gets to the edge of town, however, his mood changes. Everything looks very gloomy and foreboding, nothing like the bright colored buildings that he saw from on top. The atmosphere just feels like, well, death. After the Six Year War, this is the last thing he wants to feel.

"What in the world is that?" He asks himself.

When he gets close enough, he sees something distinctively different, a moat that stretches as far as the eye can see. Not just any moat, this one is at least 20 feet long and well over 100 feet deep. There is no water to drown enemies. Also absent are wild animals and reptiles ready to tear any intruders to shreds. It is just a giant gaping hole full of sand all the way down to abyss. The walls around this moat have been carefully dug out to be a direct 90 degree drop. Wind conditions over the years also helped smooth it out completely. There are no places to hang on to if anyone were to fall – no branches, not niches, and no signs of caves.

From the looks of it, there are only two ways of getting in. The first way is to fly in, which is out of the question. Packing light, he doesn't even have the necessary equipment to make a glider or anything that can remotely be used to go across this gaping hole. Besides, judging from the fortifications, the city probably has tons of land to air missiles waiting to shoot any unauthorized crafts to bits.

The only ways to get across on foot are simple hanging bridges made out of interwoven twine that connect the land to the rest of the world. Each bridge is only about three feet wide. There is one about every quarter of a mile around the land. Not only are the steps of each bridge far and apart, they look dangerous. The ropes are frail and weathered, as if they have not been used in years. There is also a battered looking warning sign. It has been so worn out that he can only make out a few alphabets, but he is pretty sure what it says – "KEEP OUT" in big red letters, or at least he thinks it used to be red.

On the other side of the moat are barbed wires – snarling and menacing looking ones. They definitely look much stronger than the bridge. Each strand is about 5 feet tall and each spike is no less than 6 inches long. They are definitely better maintained than the bridges. In fact, it looks like they sharpen and oil the tips on a regular basis. There is not a speck of rust to be seen. One look at it tells any and all passersby to keep going and not bother to try to get in.

One thing that is missing is a city wall. You would think a land that is so uninviting would be locked down behind a ten-foot wall and fortified with armed men all around the perimeter, but there is none to be seen. Hence, there is no door to break down and no guards either. In fact, he does not see a single person. Despite the pristine condition of the buildings within the moat, it almost seems like a ghost town from where he stands.

"Wow, Victor certainly did a number on my homeland." Trip laments.

The Algoma he remembers is friendly and open. This is the exact opposite. He wonders whether or not the Algomians have also changed. It certainly seems that way, and not for the better. It looks like they have grown to be suspicious of anyone coming their way, even visitors. How do relatives or friends visit their loved ones? Is it forbidden? Are they really that terrified of intruders that they have sheltered themselves inside all of this ridiculous defenses and cut off from the rest of the world? He certainly hopes not. It would certainly not be the Algoma that he knows.

Nevertheless, after coming all of this way, he, for one, is certainly not about to be turned away so easily. His mission remains the same. He needs to get across that bridge and find out what has happened to Algoma. Besides, he is not an outsider, per se, even though he has not been here for decades. The main question is how he will get across. He is sure the ropes will break if he tries to cross it. After analyzing the situation, he realizes that these bridges are merely out there for show. They are nothing more than a decoy to dissuade anyone from entering. There must be another way into town.

There is no way his home town is self-sufficient enough to not need to leave the and at all. Being a desert, there is just not enough natural resources to sustain everyone even though the Algomians that he remembers are very hearty people who work hard to turn their land into arable soil. From what he can see, he does not even see any livestock or farms to speak of. He distinctly recalls that many of his tribesman tended sheep and cows as well as grown corn. He has fond memories of running through them during harvest time. It was like an endless maze.

Perhaps, Algoma is in lock down. Has the security sensed a possible intruder, namely *him*? He takes out a telescope and studies the bridges to confirm his suspicions. The sign is not merely there to warn intruders, there is a tiny camera where the screw is. Someone is obviously watching him right now, trying to determine whether he is a friend or foe.

Considering that he has not been shot at, he is probably safe, for now at least. Despite the long journey, Trip has decided to travel on foot rather than using another mode of transportation that can run out of gas or get stuck along the way. It's a good thing, too, because he looks like a mere traveler. Carrying nothing more than a knapsack with only essentials such as cloth, canteen, tools, and his black bottles of meals, he looks like any other hiker. Without looking straight into his eyes, he looks quite harmless to an average person despite his completely black outfit and boots.

Then again, there is no telling how paranoid his tribesmen have become. There is a good chance that any sudden movement can prompt someone to shoot before asking questions. To be safe, he raises his hands up in the air, signaling that he comes in peace. Of course, that can also be misinterpreted. If these people are as paranoid as he fears, they may wonder how he knows to put his hands up. Nevertheless, he is hoping that someone is looking at his gestures as a friendly sign and sends an escort to take him in peacefully.

*

After waiting for what seems like an eternity, he hears the sound of an engine revving up. There is no telling what they have in mind at this point. After having to fight the Legionnaires, he is ready for anything. He is El Diablo, after all. With any luck, he can handle a few more bullet holes in him, but he really hopes it will not come to that. If it does, it would be the ultimate irony – being shot by the very people he is trying to help after surviving through so much enemy bullets.

About two feet under the hanging bridge, a ten-foot wide and three-foot thick metal bridge starts to protrude from the wall as the ground shakes thunderously. Trip is intrigued by this new technology. The Algoma he remembers does not care for such advancements, but they have to adapt. As soon as he hears the click on this side of the moat to signal that the bridge is connected, three heavy tanks drive out from behind a building. Trip is not sure where exactly they are coming from since none of the buildings that he sees seem to be big enough to house such massive machines, especially three of them.

When the first tank is about five feet from him, a massive gun comes out from the front of the tank.

"State your business," a calm voice of a man says from a loudspeaker.

"I am coming home," Trip replies with an equally unemotional voice.

19

After a long silence, the man says, "State your name."

"Trip."

There is a pause again. It appears that his name rings a bell. Perhaps, they have heard of him, but then, the man continues, "Trip? Trip What? Do you not have a last name?"

"No, I don't," he replies flatly.

Back then, things were a lot simpler. Algomians only went by first names. There was no reason to have a surname because everyone considered everyone else a member of the same family, which is also the reason why he has such an unusual name. It does not stand for anything else, is not short for another name, and is not a nickname. His parents knew that there would be many Johns or Michaels around. Because his mother loved to see other places, his parents decided to name him "Trip," which signifies something new and exciting at every turn.

The man in the tank seems to know this part of the Algomian past and decides not to press on the issue. In fact, as far as he is concerned, this is actually an excellent response, because it collaborates his story. Nevertheless, that does not mean he is ending the interrogation just yet.

Still pretending not to have never heard of Trip and keeping his poker face, he says, "There is no one by that name who lives within these perimeters. You are trespassing and you must vacate the premises immediately or you will be fired upon."

Looking straight into the only area with glass plating in it, Trip says, "You are correct. I do not live here right now, but I did 23 years ago. The last time I was here was August 27, 2068, the day I witnessed my family and friends die."

Perhaps, it's a sense of pride. Even though Trip is not a man of many words, he seems to think that it is important for these people to know where he came from and what he had endured there. There is another moment of silence. Under normal circumstances, he would have taken off already, but, not today. Nevertheless, he is getting impatient.

Then, he stares into the tank and says in a firm voice, "I am putting my hands down now while you decide whether or not to trust me" as he slowly puts lowers his hands.

Yes, there is a chance they may shoot him, but it's highly unlikely. For a member of the military or even security detail to take so many long pauses while questioning a possible intruder, it is obvious to Trip that they believe him, but want to be cautious before admitting to it.

After waiting for what seems like an eternity, the door of the tank finally opens and two armed men with an assault rifle, ski mask, and army fatigue come out. He wonders why they need to wear masks at all. Are they trying to prevent anyone from recognizing them? If so, why? Are they *really* Algomians or imposters who have taken over control of his tribe? It wouldn't be that difficult for invaders to recreate his home town. All they needed were a few Algomian hostages to provide the specifications.

"Get a hold of yourself," he chastises himself, "it's too early to speculate."

The first man to emerge says, "Let's go" as he signals Trip to walk across the bridge.

"Wow, what a welcome home this is. At least they seem to believe me or at least wants to talk with me further." Trip thinks to himself, but remains completely emotionless.

He walks calmly with the two men pointing their weapons at him. Together, they pass the tanks slowly before the giant machines reverse directions and follow them closely behind. So close that if he stops in his track, one of the tanks may actually run into him. Shaking his head

21

mentally, Trip cannot believe how unreasonably fearful his tribesmen have become. As they get to the middle of the bridge, he takes a deep but quiet breath. He has not been out in the desert for so long that he doesn't realize how much he misses the hot, dry, but fresh air with a scent that is distinctly missing from Balavan. There is no mistake, this *is* the same place.

After everyone crosses over, the bridge closes as quickly as it opens. The three men continue to walk into the first building. Inside, there is a group of men dressed exactly like his escorts. In fact, they look like clones of each other. They all have the same haircut and almost the same build and height. With masks on, the only distinguishable differences among them are their eyes, which works for Trip. Having stared into the eyes of his enemy for so many years, he has a real knack for telling them apart.

One of the escorts points to the chair in the middle and say, "Sit."

Trip casually sits down, but remains upright, just the way a professional soldier does. Then, a man walks out from the crowd and says, "I hear your name is Trip and you came from here. What are you doing back here?"

With a cold, but serious voice, he says, "Homesick."

Even though he is telling the truth, there is a reason for his seemingly callous answer. He knows those in the room do not know him well enough to know that he is sincere in his response. Instead, he expects them to take that as a sly sarcasm, which prompts a few of the men to take out their weapons. By doing so, he can tell which ones are the leaders and which ones are the subordinates.

The man who spoke earlier waves his hand to tell them to put the guns away as if he is the leader, but from the way that the town is surrounded by fake bridges, there is no telling if he is merely a decoy or the real thing. Trip scans around the room to see if there is another man who may be the *real* head of this operation. As he looks, he spots a person of interest instantly. This individual is leaning against a column very casually, has no emotions whatsoever, and is devoid of any weapons.

To the common eye, this person is merely an observer, but Trip knows better. If experience has taught him anything, this must be *the* man or perhaps woman. Despite the common outfit, it is obvious to him that this is a lady who is the true power behind it all. Trip thinks it's actually kind of funny. She sort of reminds him of Violet, again.

The man continues and says, "Please excuse their rudeness. If you are truly from here, you should understand why they are a little jumpy."

"Duly noted," Trip replies as he turns towards the young woman and he says, "Please excuse my intrusion. I know it must be strange for someone to return after 23 years. What do I need to do to prove who I am?"

Then, the man who just apologized to him a few seconds ago begins to show his obvious irritation because Trip is no longer paying attention to him. He snaps his fingers at the unwelcome guest and says, "Hello, over here. Am I boring you?"

Trip ignores the gesture. He never has any tolerance for condescending behavior like that anyways. Instead, he continues to look at the woman keenly. Of course, the men are getting more agitated with each second. Some of them are muttering their disapproval of him loudly. This time, the man does not stop them from inching closer and drawing out their guns. Trip can feel the obvious tension in the air, but does not break a sweat nor does he change his emotionless expression.

Despite the foul mood, Trip is not worried. Why should he? Just because he is surrounded by dozens of armed men with only one exit, which is being blocked by another armed man, does not mean that there is anything to *worry* about. What it does mean is that he needs to have a plan before things get out of hand. Within seconds, however, he knows the crisis is almost over. The woman in charge gives the man a quick tip of her head.

With a look of disappointment, the man whistles loudly and reluctantly says, "That's enough, everyone."

Even though the men have backed down, many of them are still snarling like animals. Not believing how *unprofessional* they are, Trip is hoping that these are just the thugs who watch the gate. If they are, it's actually quite brilliant. It's like junkyard dogs; they scare away people who should not be there.

Then, looking at Trip, the man says, "come with me" with an obvious sign of disgust.

Despite the cold welcome, Trip is glad that he has arrived. At least, he is one step closer to getting the answers he is looking for. Now, he just needs to find out what is going on.

Chapter 3: Algomian Army

As he takes Trip into the other room, there are five people there, including the woman. Each of them has taken their masks off. Once he enters the room the man also removes his and points Trip to one of the empty chairs. Then, one of the four men already sitting down starts to speak.

"I guess we should start with introductions. We already know you are Trip. My name is Drew." Then, he points at each individual as he says,
"The man you have been speaking with is Mason. This is Landon, Liam, and Graham. And, that is Simone."

As they are being introduced, Trips merely nods his head to acknowledge everyone, but remains silent. Simone smiles at his stone cold expression as if she is satisfied that he is who he says he is. In his case, no response is apparently the reaction that she is looking for.

Then, she says, "Hello, stranger. Have we met?"

She looks quite familiar. Can she be the friend who he remembers from his childhood? There is no way. It would be too coincidental. Besides, he doesn't remember a Simone. If that is indeed her, the name should ring a bell. But, then again, the girl that he remembers was a tough cookie. In addition, besides the fact that this woman is a lot more muscular, has a weathered look on her face, and is somewhat taller, she *does* have several unique features. For one thing, she has the same fiery red hair and green eyes. Not many people from Algoma, or anywhere else he has been, have those. If any woman is the leader of this outfit, it would be her.

Drew also looks somewhat familiar. Where has he seen this man before? Is he a childhood friend, too? If so, he's not a close one because Trip doesn't remember him in particular. If he remembers correctly, he knew several Drew's in his childhood. He also knew quite a few Frank's and Susan's. Unlike his parents who took the effort to give him a discernible name, many others did not. Instead, they would opt for a name that has been used in the family before, particularly grandparents. With families that have many descendants, the names often become confusing. To tell them apart, some people start to use nicknames. For example, if there are three different Drew's in a family, the youngest may be identified as Little Drew, the middle one may be known as Drewy, and the oldest one may be called Big D.

Besides, unlike Simone, this Drew does not have any real distinguishable feature. Like the rest of the men in the room, he has an oval face, brown hair, brown eyes, medium build, and a distinctive five o'clock shadow. Speaking of which, he is looking at the other three men in the room and they look like they can be brothers, down to the stubby on their faces. Perhaps, it is one of the qualifications of being in this elite group. Of course, the thought is ridiculous.

Without looking directly at her, Trip replies, "Should we have?"

While some women may be insulted that a man does not remember them, Simone is not one of them. She simply chuckles. Of course, that distinct laugh sounds awfully familiar, too. Even though her voice is much more mature than the friend that he remembers, she has a particularly gentle giggle that is both feminine and angelic.

"It's got to be her," he says to himself, but he is not about to admit it yet.

Drew then continues, "What exactly do you want with us?"

"Just want to know what happened."

"What happened when?"

It doesn't take long for Trip to see that Drew can care less what he has to say. The supposed leader of the Algomian Army has no intention of listening to him and has an even less desire to answer him. To make the conversation even more uncomfortable, the four men decide to start getting closer, as if they are swarming in and surrounding their prey.

Trip pretends not to notice and says, "You know what I am talking about."

Not liking the fact that he is not even breaking a sweat, Drew continues to play dumb and says, "No, I don't. If you want us to help you, you need to be much more forthcoming."

Trip cannot believe he has to spell it out.

Knowing that he is driving a bigger wedge between him and Drew, he says, "What makes you think I need your help?"

"Why, you, insolent...." Drew says as he draws his pistol.

Trip Standing only a few feet away from him, Trip opens his shirt and says, "Go ahead. See if you can aim."

The insult definitely touched a nerve. Fuming, Drew does not hesitate to cock his pistol as he watches Trip remain as calm and cool as ever, which makes him even angrier. Meanwhile, Simone's eyes widen and her mouth opens slightly in amazement for a split second. Sensing that things are about to turn south quickly, Simone composes herself before anyone else notices and interrupts this little game of who is the bigger man before someone ends up dead. She has a feeling that it would be Drew.

In a stern, calm, and chilling voice, she says, "I believe we have gone off the wrong road. Shall we get back to the discussion, gentlemen?"

"If I can still call you guys that," Simone thinks to herself.

Although somewhat surprised that she spoke, they both understand her meaning. Muttering under his breath, he puts away his pistol as Trip buttons his shirt back, but not before Simone got a good look at it. It's not the perfectly toned and muscular physique that caused her to be astounded. Quite the contrary, she was actually in awe because of what is *imperfect* about him.

She has heard of the rumors of El Diablo surviving three simultaneous shots to the chest with a high powered rifle and annihilating his enemy before they could reload, but she never thought she was going to see the living proof. Not only are they bullet holes, they are *huge* ones, the kind that can take out an elephant. It's like being in the same room with a legend. She is actually surprised that Drew has not noticed. Then again, perhaps, he did, which probably made him crosser.

Turning to Trip, Simone acts like she hasn't seen proof of his gallantry and says, "Please get to the point. As you can tell, we are not big fans of games."

Even though he knows that the chance is slim, he decides to give this irritating man another chance before taking him out cold, but out of respect for Simone, he is going to hold back. If he is going to play nice, he better get *something* out of him.

Taking a deep but silent breath, he says, "What happened after the tribe was burned to the ground?"

"We rebuilt it from the ground up."

Without showing his irritation, he thinks to himself, "Well, duh! What kind of stupid answer is that? The tribe is obviously rebuilt." It looks like these people are not going to give up a single bit of information out right. It seems they are too afraid to say anything just in the off chance that he may use it against them and destroy the place again. This is going to take a lot longer than he initially expected.

Not to let Drew get the satisfaction, he continues his line of questioning, "Who is *we*?"

"The Algomians."

"How many are there left?"

"We have pretty much repopulated ourselves."

Although the answers seem very useless to the common man, Trip has learned *something* out of them by reading between the lines. If he is telling the truth, no one else has invaded Algoma since Victor. Hence, the people who reconstructed the entire tribe are the original inhabitants. This also implies that they did it all by themselves without any help from outsiders.

But just to be sure, he asks, "Where did you get the funds to restore the tribe?"

"From our people."

While the other answers seem generic enough to be true, but worthless, this statement certainly raises a flag.

"How did our people still have the money if everything was burned down?" Trip asks suspiciously.

"There are those who returned home after finding out about the tragedy."

This answers sounds too good to be true. Considering that the Algomians are very simple people, there couldn't possibly have been that many of expatriates who have the kind of money to reestablish the entire tribe. Nevertheless, he decides not to press the issue any further for now. Besides, even if he asks, it is not likely that Drew knows the *real* answer anyways.

Changing the subject, he asks, "Where is everyone?"

"Where they always are."

"And where is that?"

"In their homes."

By now, even Simone is starting to smile at the ridiculous back and forth banter. Why cannot Drew just give a straight answer, which will speed up the conversation by leaps and bounds? On the hand, judging from her amusement, this seems very typical for the man. By her silence, Trip can tell that she is also not going to divulge anything helpful. Sensing that he probably can get much better answers from her, he decides to call it a day.

"Is there a hotel nearby?"

"Yes."

After a few seconds of silence, Trip's sarcasm is in full force as he spells it out for him again slowly, "Can you direct me to it?"

"No."

"Where can I stay for the night?"

"You cannot."

Showing a sign of smugness, the four men seem to enjoy playing this game. They are obviously taunting him with their eyes and asking, "What's your next move, stranger? Are you going to leave yet? Should we taunt you some more?"

Since it is highly unlikely that Trip is the only one who has ever tried to visit the place, Drew probably has done this many times before to those who have not been scared away from the foreboding looking fortifications. After being intimated, most of them probably simply give up and leave with no intention of ever returning.

It's plain to see that is not the case with Trip. Drew is getting an uneasy feeling about this latest intruder. He is wondering why he is not more frustrated than he appears.

In fact, it looks like he intends to stay. He is even starting to ask himself whether or not he is more than meets the eye. Before he tries to hatch a plan to get rid of him, however, Trip knows that this is a lost cause and excuses himself.

"Thank you for your hospitality," Trip says with a bit of sarcasm. He nods at Simone and starts to head back to the bridge.

*

As he gets right on the edge, the bridge automatically opens without his asking. At least they know how to get rid of people quickly. Before he finishes crossing the bridge, he can hear snickering in the back. Trip cannot believe how childish the leaders of the new Algomian Army are. He is more than a little disappointed at the turn of events. It's one thing for them to be extremely paranoid. It's another to act this way towards visitors, especially someone who is *from* there.

The only saving grace is Simone. He knows that the key to understanding what happened lies solely on her. Just like the initial meeting they had with Mason, Trips is convinced that she is the real leader behind the blabbering idiots. Knowing that she is the only one who is not congratulating herself at that moment, Trip is deliberately showing her where he is going. Having seen where the cameras are on the bridges, he figures out which areas is safe from prying eyes. Then, he pitches himself the same tent that he has made since he started the journey. Now, it's just a matter of time before she comes to him.

After setting up camp, Trip lies on the ground to watch the sunset and enjoying the cool and crisp breeze. Surrounded by the wild flowers from his youth, he cannot believe how wonderful it feels and smells out here. Fond memories are flooding back to him as a slight smile is appearing on his lips. Despite the horrible treatment that he received earlier that day, *this* is what makes it all worthwhile. *This* is why he has come home.

As he closes his eyes to take it all in with his other senses, he hears soft footsteps calmly coming towards him.

"Hello, Simone," he says without opening his eyes.

"I guess it's pretty obvious that it's me, huh?"

"Yes."

"So, am I talking to the legendary El Diablo?"

"Ah, so you *have* heard of me."

"Of course. We all have. Trip is an uncommon name. We knew who you are the minute we heard you utter your name. You are a hero among these people."

There's *we* again. It sounds like the new Algomian Army does everything in groups. Ordinarily, this is not a bad thing, but in this case, Trip is wondering if the leaders are merely agreeing with one another out of peer pressure rather than consensus. Even though Simone is the only one who is not a mere clone of the others, Trip wonders why she does not speak up when Drew speaks and why she has to sneak out in the middle of the night to come see him. There is no time better than now to ask.

"Well, that's a strange way to treat a hero," Trip replies as he tries to steer the conversation towards the rest of the group.

32

"I know. I am sorry about the way Drew treated you today. He does that to everyone."

"Why?"

"He doesn't like anyone new."

"Well, that much is obvious."

"And, more importantly," Simone says as she gets more serious, "He is afraid that you are a traitor."

"Why would he think that?"

"I don't know, exactly. Insecurity? Paranoia? Arrogance? Pick one."

"So, why are you with him?"

"Oh, I am not."

"Well, you are certainly not *against* him."

Smiling, she says, "OK, let me correct my statement. Yes, I work with him, but not for him."

"That is also obvious."

"Yes, I sense that you already figured that out, too."

"So what are you not telling me?"

By leaving the question open, he is testing to see if she is willing to divulge any information or if she is just like Drew, but a nicer and less sarcastic version. As he studies her expression, she starts to blush. Trip is not sure if she is embarrassed before he is staring into her eyes or something else.

"Where should I start?" she asks after quickly recomposing herself.

"Anywhere you want."

Taking out her golden snapdragon necklace, she asks, "Remember this?"

Simone's parents had given her that necklace for her tenth birthday, merely two months before Algoma was destroyed. Shortly after receiving it, she showed it to Trip who complemented it, which is something he did not, and still does not, do very often. She knows that if he remembers anything about her, it would be this necklace and she is right. He has always loved golden snapdragons and the detailed craftsmanship on the pendant was absolutely exquisite.

It was the last thing that she received from her loving parents before they were massacred with the rest of the tribesmen. She has never taken it off. Over the years, it still retains its beauty around her neck. Like Trip, she became an orphan that day, along with dozens of other children who were deemed too weak and too insignificant to kill. Even though she has lost everything else, she has always made sure that she has kept it safe and close to her heart.

"Yes," Trip admits. So it *is* her, but for the life of him, he doesn't recall ever having a Simone as a friend.

Smiling, Simone says, "You look confused."

"No, why do you say that?"

"Let me guess, even though you remember me, you don't remember my name."

Since she calls him out on his, he no longer bothers to hide it as he nods.

"How about Cici? Does that name sound more familiar?"

"Why do you call yourself Simone?"

"Because that's the name my mother gave me."

"Why is it I didn't know that back then?"

Laughing, she says, "You don't remember?"

Shaking his head, Trip is trying to think back there, but nothing is coming to mind.

"You told me you didn't like that name. So, you started calling me Cici because you thought I was silly."

Now, he remembers. Yes, that was the day they met. The two of them were playing in the desert, ignoring each other until she accidentally bumped into a cactus. Trying to be brave, she did not cry and would not admit that she was in pain. Instead, she did this really goofy series of moves and pretended that she was dancing.

Trip started to laugh but after seeing the needles stuck to her, he went over and helped get them out. After they finally removed every one of them, she introduced herself, but Trip insisted on calling her Cici instead. He was the only one who ever called her that. From that day forward, they were best friends until that disastrous day.

"So, what happened to you after that day?" Simone asks.

"I survived." Trip replies.

Simone is somewhat disappointed that he is not willing to open up to her, but it's to be expected. Although he was a happy person as a child, she heard the rumors about El Diablo and knows that he has gone through a great deal. She understands if he does not want to dig up bitter memories, but she figures it doesn't hurt to ask, but knows better than to press.

"Well, I am sure you can tell me more when the time is right," she says with an understanding nod. Then, she continues, "Your turn. What do you want to ask me? I figure you are on a personal mission to get some answers. Otherwise, you wouldn't have come this way without any backup."

"Who really rebuilt this land?" Trip asks immediately.

35

"Drew was telling the truth. We all did. It took many years. There were only about 50 survivors, mostly children. Drew was among the oldest. He was eleven."

"How does an eleven year old lead 50 children on a burned out land with nothing to eat or drink?" Trip asks dubiously.

"He didn't start out as the leader. He wandered off the land, too, much like yourself. But, he came back within three days with a wagon full of food, water, and tools."

"Where did he get them?"

"We don't know. He would never say. He merely told us that there is a person who used to be from Algoma who donated them. It was not a moment too soon. Many of the children were too young and fragile to last another day."

"How did he say he found this person?"

"Apparently, when the war broke out, this person heard about it and was on the way to help when he ran into Drew."

"What's his name?"

"You know better than to ask that question. Drew would never give us a name. All he said was that the benefactor prefers to remain anonymous."

"No one tried to question him?" Trip asks curiously.

"Why would anyone? When you are faced with certain death, the source is hardly important. We were all desperate. Besides, we were all too young to care."

"I don't mean on that day."

"I figured, but, no, no one bothered to ask because it would sound like we were ungrateful. After the dust finally settled and everyone began to heal, all they could think about was how grateful they were to Drew. Many of them literally owed their lives to him. He became an instant sensation among the survivors. Everyone wanted to be his friend. Needless to say, he became our leader that day even though he didn't want to be one."

"Sounds familiar," Trip says to himself before asking "What about you?"

"What about me?"

"He seems to have an unusual fondness for you. Have you tried to question him? I am sure if he trusts anyone, it would be you."

"You would think so, but the non-answers that he gave you earlier are quite typical for him. I knew he was never going to tell me anyways. So, I didn't ask." Simone confesses.

"Have you tried to find out?"

"Of course. I have reviewed security tapes and have been watching him for years, but he is very good at covering his tracks, kind of like you," she says slyly.

Smiling, Trip thinks it's funny that she goes behind his back like that. If she is as important to him as it appears, why does she need to sneak around? They definitely have an interesting relationship.

"How much does he trust you?" Trip asks with a good amount of curiosity.

"More than anyone else, but that doesn't say much."

"Does he know you are talking with me?"

"Probably. Even though he holds many secrets, he does not like it when someone else has them. I know he watches every one of us very closely."

"Ah," Trip says to himself. He gets it now. It's a two-way street. He doesn't trust her so she doesn't trust him. It's sad really. He is glad his relationship with Violet is much more open and honest. He would hate to be Drew – so fearful and sad.

"It sounds to me that he is not merely hiding information because he doesn't trust anyone. Do you suspect that he may be hatching something sinister?"

"Well, he's been like this for 23 years and he has not done anything bad yet. At least not something that is detrimental to Algoma."

"Interesting disclaimer at the end. What has he done that might be considered bad, but not bad enough to be considered detrimental?"

Laughing, Simone says, "I wasn't implying anything specific, but you got me. I have seen him do things that are bad for morale and may be somewhat questionable, but never anything illegal."

"Like what?"

"Really? You are really going to make me say it?"

"Yes."

Although Trip normally doesn't pry, somehow it seems OK to do so with her. It's almost like old times. He would tease her and she would get back at him.

"Well, I am sorry to disappoint you, but I have my reasons to decline," Simone says with a sad smile.

With that short sentence, Trip is back to reality. It is not like the old days. She has definitely matured. It has been over two decades. Everyone changes with time. He doesn't blame her, but he cannot honestly say that he is not disappointed. He had hoped to be able to connect with home at some level. Oh, well, guess that takes time, too.

Turning more serious, he says, "You don't think this lack of trust is bad?"

Nodding, she says, "I don't like it, but we all learn to live with his rules because none us would be here today if it wasn't for him."

"Second question: where is everyone else?"

"Ah, you noticed. The town you see above ground is nothing more than a decoy. The Algomians live underground."

"That explains why they are not worried about people flying into town. They cannot. That's actually pretty smart and quite deceptive," Trip says to himself before saying, "Don't you think this is a little overboard?"

"Yes, but it is practical. Since we are a desert land, it does get quite hot up here. By going underground, we can get our water much easier and safer."

"What about farming or do you not do that anymore?"

"We use artificial lighting, but you couldn't really tell if you have never come up to the surface. It's quite ingenious. To the people living down there, it's like having the real sun, which rises in the east and sets in the west every day. We even have regular rain for the crops and strategically placed fans that simulate wind. The best thing is we can control the weather to be perfect, unlike out here where we are often at the mercy of Mother Nature," Simone says proudly.

"How many people live down there?"

"Instead of telling you, why don't I show you?"

Surprised at the offer, Trip says with an obvious tone of sarcasm, "How are you going to get Drew to allow an *outsider* to take a tour?"

"Like I said, I don't answer to him."

"Dare I ask why? From what you said so far, it sounds like *everyone* answers to him."

"Everyone but me. I am his wife." Simone replies with a grin.

For a split second, Trip actually looks shocked. *That* is about the only piece of information that he is not expecting, but logically, it should not have come as a surprise. After all, they have been working close together for two decades. At the very least, it explains a lot. For example, it confirms his assumption that she is the real power behind the face. At the same time, Trip is a little more wary of Drew than before.

If he does not tell his own wife who the benefactor is, this is serious business and highly suspicious. What and who is he really hiding? At the same time, he feels for Simone more than ever before. What kind of marriage is it if there is no trust? He can never imagine being in a relationship like that. As far as he is concerned, a matrimony should be between two people who will die for one another and put each another ahead of anyone else.

Patting him on the shoulder, she says, "Oh, come on, this shouldn't change anything. It's still me you are talking to."

For a second, it almost seems like he is talking with Violet.

Almost as if she can read his mind, she says, "Surely you are married to the Warrior."

Embarrassed, Trip simply blushes as he vehemently denies it.

"No, of course not! Why would you even suggest such a ridiculous thing?"

This is the first time anyone has even mentioned the notion. Despite having spent so much time with Violet, he has not once entertained the idea of marriage. He wonders if Violet has ever thought of it. After knowing each other since they were children, he has always thought of her as his annoying, albeit loving and kind-hearted, younger sister.

There is no doubt that he would die for her and she would do the same for him. It's also true that he finds her quite attractive. Despite is propensity for darkness, he enjoys her bubbly personality, too. It's like they complement each other perfectly. Yet, the topic has never come up. Perhaps, she has been waiting for him to start even though she knows that he would never bring up a topic like that.

Laughing, Simone says, "You haven't changed one bit."

Leading him back towards town, she says, "Come on, before you die of embarrassment."

As he follows her dutifully, he has to ask, "Why did you marry him?"

"Why not?"

"Do you love him?"

"That's kind of a personal question, don't you think?"

"Oh, come on, don't cop out on me now. You have to avoiding my questions the entire time. Has he really robbed that much off of you?" Trip says, teasing her as he once did.

"No, I don't love him, but we make good partners. People listen to him, but he doesn't always have the best ideas, if you know what I mean," she admits as she raises her left eyebrow.

Nodding, Trip is all too familiar with this arrangement. It's almost exactly the same as the relationship he has with Violet with the difference that he is not as much of a mean-spirited fool as Drew is. At least, he hopes he doesn't come across as one.

"Does he know?"

"No, nobody does. I don't even know why I told you – probably because you are the only with the guts to ask."

41

Smirking, Trip is glad that she answered him. Before he gets the chance to celebrate, whoever, she comes back with a question.

"Now that I answered a personal question, I think you owe me an answer."

Looking grim, Trip knows what she wants to hear and finally agrees to tell her about how Violet's family saved him so long ago. Even without the details, Simone can picture it exactly the way it happened. She did not realize that he wandered alone for so long in the hot sand at such a young age. All of this time, she thought he had gotten lucky and was saved by a soldier immediately after the war. That is how she explained his extraordinary skills on the battlefield. She had never thought that he became who he is by suffering so much. As if she was not already impressed with El Diablo, she now has an increased sense of admiration for him.

At the same time, she also understands why he has not married Violet. He probably can never repay her for saving his life. Hence, he always keeps a distance from her in order to put her up on the pedestal. He is probably also afraid that taking their relationship up a notch may ruin what they already have. Patting him on the back, Simone gives him an understanding smile.

Trip is glad to see that there is a part of her that hasn't changed at all – her ability to understand him as well as her honesty towards him. With her by his side, he confident that he has a fighting chance to survive whatever it is he is facing in the new Algoma.

Chapter 4: Uneasy Feeling

Going to a different side of the moat, Simone pushes a discreet button behind the warning sign. Immediately, a metal pole comes up on the right side of the sign before a simple metal panel opens up. As she puts her palm on it, a blue light scans it and a clear, almost invisible bridge silently comes out from the cliff. With each step, the bridge extends a little longer until they reach across the moat to the other side of the cliff.

As expected, there is a door at the end that is difficult to see until he gets within a foot of it. As they get right up to it, it opens. Inside is nothing but a very small spherical room that is about five feet in diameter and six feet tall, which looks like an elevator, but with no visible buttons or markings of any kind. As soon as she enters, the bridge seems to disappear, but he knows it's nothing but a clever trick of the eye. Then, she simply stands there as if she is waiting for him to see everything before moving on to make sure that he remembers all of the details. He can hear the light humming sound of the bridge retracting quickly until it clicks softly on the other side, signaling that it has withdrawn completely.

As she watches his reactions, Simone smiles lightly and says, "Impressed?"

Even though he nods, she knows that he doesn't mean it. Although he is awestruck at how far his hometown has come technologically and architecturally, he is more disappointed with the reasons behind the need for these advancements than anything else. Satisfied that he has seen enough of the way in, she waves her hand over a discrete looking bump on the wall and the door closes and they start to descend quickly.

When the door opens, Trip is surprised how beautiful it is inside. All of the buildings look exactly like the way he remembers. It seems the new residents spare no expense to get every detail right, from the colorful walls and the layout of the tribe to the flowers and the rivers. It's as if he has returned home. For a second, he has to ask: Was it all a nightmare? After taking it all in, he comes back to reality.

He knows perfectly well that it wasn't. After all, they *are* underground. Remembering where his childhood home was, he quickly walks in that direction. Even though he knows it's nothing but a replication, he has to see it. As he gets closer, he cannot believe it. There it is – exactly the way he remembers it. It's almost too cruel.

Stopping right in front of it, Trip looks very solemn and asks, "Who lives there?"

"A lovely family," Simone says.

"Can I go in and take a look?"

"I don't see why not."

Hesitating for a second, Trip finally raises his fist to knock on the door.

"Who is it?" a little girl says from inside as the sound of her little feet patters lightly on the wooden floor inside.

"It's Simone."

As the door swings open, the cheerful girl runs to her and gives her a big hug and says, "Hi, Auntie Simone! What took you so long to come back and see us?"

Then, she drags her inside the house while Trip stands there just looking sadly. Not recognizing the child, Trip no longer feels comfortable going in. Although the house looks like home, seeing a stranger, albeit a cute little one, inside of it reminds him that it is *not* home.

"Are you coming in?" Simone asks.

Shaking his head, Trip says, "I will just wait out here for you."

Knowing that Trip really wants to see it, Simone tries to encourage him.

"Tiffany, I want you to meet a very old friend of mine. This is Trip," Simone says to the little girl.

Taking out her tiny little hand like a big girl, Tiffany says, "Hi, Mr. Trip. I am Tiffany. It's lovely to meet you!"

Trip has never been offered a hand to shake from a little girl before. In fact, he has not been around little children since he was one himself. Being dark and gloomy, he has never found himself to be good around the younger generation. They usually run away from him as soon as they see him. This little girl is different. She doesn't look scared at all. She has a very bright and cheerful glow in her big round green eyes, which looks very much like Simone's.

Kneeling down on one knee, Trip takes out his hand to shake hers and says, "Hello, Tiffany. It's nice to meet you, too."

Even though he tries to be as gentle as he can, Trip really doesn't know how to speak to a child. Despite his best efforts, his voice is deep and dark and his face remains emotionless. Tiffany's eyes turn from a joyous look to a concerned one.

"Why you are so sad, Mr. Trip?" Tiffany asks.

Surprised that she calls him out on it, Trip says, "Oh, no, I am not sad."

"Yes, you are. You know, when I feel sad, a cookie always makes me feel better. Want one?"

"No, that's ok. I don't want to intrude."

"Oh, don't worry, you are not intruding! They are *really* good! Mommy just baked them an hour ago."

45

He feels his heart wrench a little when she said that. He remembers his mother used to love to bake, too. She made the most decadent treats, especially her Goji berry cookies. While everyone else made sugar cookies, his mom would make different kinds for him from all types of native berries that he could find. It started out with him picking a bunch of them from the road when he was a mere toddler. He couldn't get enough of them. Before long, they have a garden full of different kinds of berries like the Wolfberries, Soapberries, and the Red Barberries. Knowing how much he liked them, she started putting them in all of her desserts.

As he reminisces, he doesn't realize that Tiffany has already pulled him in inside the house. Just as he thought, the layout of the house is exactly the same as he remembers. Of course, the rooms look a little smaller, probably because he has gotten bigger. At the same time, he can tell that it is not his home. While the furniture is the same style, they are arranged differently. Although the cookies do smell good as he gets closer to the kitchen, it's not the same aroma as the ones his mother used to bake.

"Hi, Mommy," Tiffany shouts as she drags Trip into the kitchen. "This is Trip. He's my new friend. Can he have a cookie?"

Tiffany's mother stops in her track, turns around, and simply stares at him for a moment. Like every other adult in Algoma, she has heard of Trip, the legendary El Diablo, but from her reaction, whatever she thinks of him is definitely not good.

"Hello," Tiffany's mom says indifferently as she grabs her daughter close.

Recognizing the cold shoulder, Trip says, "I apologize for the intrusion, ma'am. I shall be going," before turning around to leave.

"No! No! Please don't go yet!" Tiffany shouts as she frees herself from her mother's grasp to pull him back.

"Tiffany!" her mother shouts.

Knowing that she is in trouble, Tiffany lets go and says, "Bye, Mr. Trip. I hope to see you again soon."

As Trip walks towards the door, Simone follows him. He can feel Tiffany's mother's icy gaze on him, judging him, and waiting for him to leave. As soon as they exit, she hurries to lock the door behind them. Despite the closed door, he can hear lecturing her confused daughter. He feels sorry for poor Tiffany, who was only trying to be nice to him. She seems to be the only one who has made him feel welcome since he first laid eyes on the new Algoma.

"Wait," Simone says as she hurries behind him.

Ignoring her, he quickens his pace to go back towards the elevator.

"Are you really going to give up and run back home before you find you are looking for?"

If Simone thinks those words will stop him, she is dead wrong. He has never cared for insults regardless of whether or not she indented them to be one. Instead, it actually encourages him to go even faster to the point where she has to run after him.

"Please, will you listen to me for a second?" she starts to plead. "For old time sake."

Now, those last four words catch his attention. Although he does not say a word, he has slowed his pace so she can catch up to him.

"Can you please come with me so I can explain?"

Going behind what looks like a garbage bin, there is a door there. Waving her hand over a spot, a door opens to a familiar looking elevator. As quickly as they descended, they ascended back up to the surface. As the door opens, he finds himself in a quaint little house. It looks exactly like a home complete with common pieces of furniture in every room. At the same time, it looks like no one lives in it. It must be a meeting place when the Algomian Army wants to discuss important matters.

Sitting down on a sofa, Simone says, "Please rest assured. There is no surveillance in this house. We can be open and honest."

Not believing her completely, Trip looks around at every fixture to see if there are pinhole cameras. Although he is not convinced that there are none, he no longer cares.

"What do you want from me?" he says coldly.

"I am sorry you have to endure that. I figure it will be easier to show you our new home than to tell it to you."

Pretending not to notice the icy atmosphere towards him, Trip coldly says, "There is no need to apologize."

Smiling, Simone says, "At least, you are talking to me again."

Of course, those words merely shuts him back up again as he waits for her to explain herself as she has promised to do.

Clearing her throat, she continues, "I know you must have felt unwelcome down there even though I gave you cause to expect otherwise. I assure you I was not lying to you nor was I trying to flatter you when I told you that you are a hero amongst our people. You were, or are. It's just that after you didn't show up after twenty years, people start to wonder if you are real or not. Before long, rumors started floating that you were a coward who ran away from the tribe when your people needed you the most. By now, you are more *infamous* there than famous, but that is definitely unwarranted."

Sensing that those words cut him deep, she tries to soften the blow and says, "Many of us still believe you are a hero. Come on! You defeated the man who destroyed our home. How can you not be one?"

Instead of making him feel better, she is actually doing just the opposite. Now, it sounds like she is merely patronizing him.

Realizing that she is still not getting to him, she says, "Even though you did technically leave the tribe, it's not like you could have defended us when you were seven. Having a fierce reputation like yours is a double edged sword. On one hand, many people place great hopes in you. On the other hand, you become a villain in many of their eyes if you don't show up when they expect you to."

"What do you want from me?" Trip repeats himself as he begins to put up a wall around himself.

By now, he is sure that she has a hidden agenda.

"It doesn't have to be like this. We can be friends like we were before."

Looking straight into her eyes, Trip says, "I wanted to see whether or not I can help the people of Algoma after all of these years. From what I have seen, it seems like everyone is doing just fine without me. Since I am not needed, I am going to take my leave now."

"I beg you, please don't leave."

"Give me a reason not to."

Looking a little sheepish, Simone hesitates as she tries to decide what to say.

After about a minute of silence, Trip gets up and says flatly, "Well, it was good to see you again."

"OK, OK. I will tell you, but please keep this between us," Simone says as she reaches to grab his hand, which brings back memories for both of them.

When they were little, their hands would sometimes touch when they would lie on the meadow together watching the blue skies. They would always blush and take their hands away without saying a word. At first, it was immediate. As time went by, their hands would linger a little longer before it became too awkward. As before, after a few silence moments, Trip slowly withdraws his from under hers and sits back down.

"Have you wondered how the rumor started?" Simone asks rhetorically.

Trip is not the type of speculate. Besides, he can care less what other people think of him. There is only one person's opinion that matters to him today and that is Violet.

"Drew started it. He has always been jealous of you and he cannot allow you to hold a higher esteem in the eyes of the Algomians than he does. You understand?" Simone confesses.

It comes as no surprise. Trip has figured that Drew does not like him even though he has never done anything to him. After being absent for 23 years, what can he have ever done to the man to deserve his wrath? In either case, he cannot help it if someone has an irrational hatred for him.

"I don't know if you remember him or not, but he used to hang out with us sometimes."

Trying to think back to see which one of the boys he might have been, Trip simply cannot pinpoint a face.

"He is four years older than you. Back then, he was a lot bigger than you. He was really tall and skinny at the time, and kind of awkward," Simone says with a giggle.

"He would also hide behind cacti sometimes just to watch us."

"Oh, him," Trip says as he vaguely remembers a creepy boy who would always follow them around, but rarely ever said anything or did anything with them.

"He was pretty shy at the time, which made it even harder for him to assume the leadership position when he was thrown into the spotlight. When everyone was clamoring for him to help them, he himself looked very helpless, but wouldn't admit it. I felt so bad for him that I had to help him," Simone continues.

"And, that's how you became partners," Trip says, finishing her thought.

Smiling, Simone says, "That's about right."

Shaking his head, Trip says, "Well, it's nice that I know a little bit more about your strange husband's problems, but I don't think it's any of my business."

Before he can get back up, Simone turns serious and says, "I think he's hatching something bad. I don't know what it is, but he's hiding something."

"From what I know of the man so far, that sounds like just another day for him. What else is new?"

"He's been amassing a lot of weapons recently. Since we are in isolation and have no enemies, I don't know why he is doing it."

At least, that gets Trip's attention.

"But you have an idea, don't you?" Trip says.

Nodding, she says, "I think he is planning on attacking a neighboring country."

"Why would he do that?"

"I don't know, but he has been secretly meeting with a person dressed in black just outside of town. It's always in the middle of the night when he thinks I am asleep."

"And?"

"I followed him a couple of times, but I have never been able to get close enough to hear what they say."

"What does this have to do with me?"

"I am not sure, but it's just a gut feeling. When I saw the way he looked at you, I get the sense that it somehow has to do with you."

"How?"

"I cannot put my finger on it, but he seems very irritated, more so than usual, like you are going to upset his plan."

"Maybe he just doesn't like me," Trip says as he discounts her for paranoia.

"No, it's more than that. I am sure of it – considering the timing."

"What of it?"

"For 17 years after the Great War of 2068, Drew was focused on rebuilding Algoma. There was not a day that went by that he did not talk it. He was very excited every time something was finished. Even though he didn't rebuild the tribe by himself, he often got the credit. The people showered him with gifts and gratitude, which made him happy and quite pleasant to be around. He would be caring and considerate," Simone says as she reminisces the good times.

"Was that when you married him?"

Startled by the question, she says, "Yes, we have been married for ten years now. The first few years were wonderful. He was a caring husband and father."

"Father? You have children?" Trip asks in surprise.

Even though he knows that they are married, the thought of children never entered his mind. When he thought they were childless, it was nothing more than a convenient partnership. Now, the entire dynamics of the marriage has changed. Now, they are actually a *family*.

"Yes, I have an eight year daughter named Brittany and a six year old son named Bryce," she says as she beams with pride.

"When they were born, Drew was beside himself. He would stay up with them, feed them, bathe them, and sing to them like the greatest father on earth. We couldn't be happier. Then, things turned south one day after he had one of those secret meetings. He wouldn't tell me who he met or what they discussed, but it was obvious that whatever he heard affected him a great deal. Then, he heard about the Six Year War in Balavan and the mighty El Diablo and his partner the Warrior. From then on, everything changed. He was moody and bitter. He also began to keep a distance from his family, even his own children."

"I am so sorry," Trip says sincerely, "I don't mean to sound callous, but I still don't see how any of this is my business."

"Don't you see? Whoever he has been meeting with in secret must be from Balavan. And, it seems clear, at least to me, that this person is plotting against you and your precious Violet and Drew is a part of it. I cannot tell if he is a reluctant participant or a willing one, but he is definitely involved."

"What do you have in mind?"

Smiling, Simone says, "Thank you."

Chapter 5: Clearer Picture

"Come on, the first order of business is to get you a place to stay without arousing Drew's suspicion," Simone says as she gets up to leave.

"Wait, I don't work that way. I am not going to hide like a rat. Never have. Never will. If you want me to help you, it will be open and honest."

Stopping in her track, she says, "I am sorry. I didn't mean for you to feel like a vermin. It's just that if he catches wind of something like this, he is going to stop it before we get a chance to accomplish anything. He may even throw you in prison."

"If he is the kind of person I think he is, he may even throw you in prison."

Simone looks surprised at his comment. It seems the thought has never crossed her mind. After all of this time, she has believed that their love is strong enough to weather anything, but she knows Trip is right. That may have been true in the beginning, but in the past five years, things have definitely become strained. Even though he has never raised a hand against her, she can tell that he gets irritated by her for little things that never mattered to him before. In a way, they are now business partners more than anything else. They seem to be married in only name.

"What do you suggest?" Simone asks earnestly.

"That's a tough one. Usually, Violet figures these things out."

"Why don't we ask her?"

"I cannot do that. She's much needed back home, especially in my absence."

Nodding, she says, "I understand."

"Do you have anyone else that you can trust in your group?"

"Hold on, there. I can trust a lot of people in my group. They are all good people."

"Sorry. I didn't mean to imply that they are incompetent or anything like that. Let me rephrase that. Is there anyone you can trust who is not afraid of your husband?"

"Well, *afraid* is a harsh word. Everyone here *respects* him, but I see where you are going with that. As you have already witnessed, when we are faced with a stranger, we look like we have a common front."

"You mean, you look like clones."

Laughing, Simone says, "Exactly! We are doing it right, then! We want to look the same for a good reason. If the stranger intends on targeting a leader, they wouldn't know which one of us it is!"

"Or, rather, you look like you have a group of robots who are easy picking, because they only do as they are told and have no ideas of their own."

"Wow, that's harsh! Nobody has ever said it like that before. I guess no one dares to criticize the Elders. But, once again, I see your point."

"The Elders? Wow, that makes me feel old."

Even though she knows he means it as a joke, Simone cannot help but feel sad by the statement. While everyone on her team is in the 30's, they are the oldest ones in town. It's a gloomy reminder of the Great War of 2086.

Seeing her expression, Trip says, "I apologize. I did not mean to upset you."

"Don't worry about it. Let's get back to your question," Simone says with renewed sense of purpose. "I am not sure if you remember, but among those four whom you call clones is a man named Landon. He's a dear friend of mine. I think he's trustworthy. There is also Liam. He's my cousin. He is also Tiffany's father. I know his wife didn't look very friendly when we went to their house earlier. Rest assured, it was all an act. Just like our little show when you first met us, we all have been taught to act aloof when facing a stranger."

"Well, congratulations. You have trained her well. She certainly fooled me."

"I know it's not the best tactic, but it's a necessary evil."

"Is it really?"

"You know, of all of the people in this world, I would think you would understand," Simone says disappointedly.

"Oh, I do. I just think there's a better way to do it."

Simone smiles and says, "That's why I need your help!"

Trip is confused by her reaction. He expected her to be insulted by his comment. Instead, she is excited about it. Is it all a test to see what he really thinks of the new Algoma? It certainly looks that way.

"Hold on. Before we get back to that again, why don't you tell me a little more about this Liam and Landon?"

"What about them?"

"If you trust these two to have your back, why don't you ask them to help?"

"They are already in too deep. If either one of them does anything out of the ordinary, Drew can sniff them out instantly. I cannot risk that."

"So, what? Since I am not in it yet, I am dispensable?"

"No, that's not what I mean! You are twisting my words!" Simone says as she starts to pout.

Waiting for her to dig herself out of the hole she has dug, Trip sits back with a grin.

56

"What I mean is that since he does not know your habits yet you are an experienced fighter, you are in the perfect position to help us."

Getting tired of the conversation, Trip sighs and asks, "Fine, now what?"

"How about we compromise? Since you don't want to be in hiding, would you mind being in disguise?"

"What kind of disguise?" Trip asks with a raised eyebrow.

"Nothing crazy. I am not talking about dressing you up in drag or anything," Simone says as she laughs. "You will still look exactly like you, but dressed as a local."

"That's not much of a disguise."

"Well, I need you to blend in and be exactly what you are, an Algomian."

"I am not sure what that will accomplish since many people already know my true identify."

"That may be true, but majority of the people do not."

"So, what exactly do you have in mind?"

"I am hoping that you can do a little undercover work for us."

"With the kind of surveillance you have, why would you need me to do that?"

"It's exactly because we have such extensive surveillance that I need you. There is simply too much information that is being captured on camera. It's getting to the point where we no longer have the ability to monitor everything," Simone explains. Then, she pauses and says, "Besides, I am not trying to spy on our own citizens. I am more interested in the ones from the outside, particularly the ones who Drew is meeting."

"Ah, the truth finally comes out. What you really want is for me to spy on your own husband."

"Well, it sounds bad when you put it that way, but, yes, that's pretty much it."

Still not convinced that he wants to be a part of it, Trip says, "You don't need me for that. You need a private investigator."

"I have tried that, but the man I hired has since disappeared."

"When?"

"I hired him about six months ago. That is how I know that Drew has been meeting in secret. At first, it was just a hunch. Over the last six months, he has confirmed that my husband has been meeting the same stranger in different places about once a week, usually at 1AM. Then, about three weeks ago, my private investigator just vanishes. I have searched all of the cameras. There is no trace of him. There is also no missing person's report."

"Let me guess. He is a loner who has no family or friends who can report him missing."

Nodding, she admits, "That's why I chose him."

"Have you searched his home?"

"Yes, there is nothing. It still has that lived in look, but everything is clean. The bed is made. The dishes are put away. There is no trash or dirty laundry."

"What about what's missing? Did he pack? Is his toothbrush still there?"

"I didn't think to look for those kinds of things, but I was in a hurry that day. If you care to join me, I think this would be the perfect time to check it out again."

"I am not agreeing to anything if I do."

"Understood," Simone says with a crooked smile.

Trip remembers what that look says. Every time she has something else in mind, she always had that look – the more crooked it is, the more sinister her plan. This looks like a *very* crooked smile.

*

Going into another brightly colored house, she goes to one of the walls in the bedroom and waves her hand in front of another camouflaged button, just like before. As the elevator opens, they ride it back into Algoma.

Looking around, Trip does not like what he see and asks, "Where are we?"

Giving him an understanding look, Simon says, "The place that you saw earlier is the area where all of the Algomians live. This is our testing area, where we make sure that everything is safe and ready for use before we move it. Only select people know about this place, the engineers, tester, etc. It's on a strictly need-to-know basis."

This place is nothing like the other one. Instead of a copy of a sunny and breezy desert, it looks like a damp underground factory. There is no sun or rivers. It looks dark and gloomy. The only source of light is artificial lamps staggered in various places.

Instead of the bubbling sound of the brook, it's the repetitive sounds of dripping from several leaky pipes. Instead of the fresh scent of flowers, the air is foul. Even though there are no obvious piles of trash or feces, it certainly smells like grease oil and raw sewage. It's no wonder that Simone and the other Elders do not want their regular citizens to get near this place. It would definitely crash morale.

There are several sections, seemingly grouped by function. In one section are houses that are unfinished or in different stages of demolition. In another section, there are various vehicles ranging from commercial ones like trains to military types like tanks and even aircrafts, which certainly capture Trip's attention. A third area is filled with different types of machineries, such as massive air conditioning systems, some of which are so huge that they are several stories tall.

"Why are you showing me this? I thought we are going to see your private investigator's home. What did you say his name is again?" Trip asks.

"I didn't. Because we go by code names, I didn't see a point of giving you a fake one unless you ask. Since you have, I call him Pete and he calls me Val, but it's solely for identification purposes."

Laughing, Trip says, "So, you know where he lives, but not his real name. Sounds to me like he doesn't actually live there. It's just a place for him to crash."

"I suspect as much. That certainly helps explain why his house was so neat, which is pretty rare for a single man living by himself," Simone says with a grin.

"So, does he live down here?"

"No, no one actually lives down here. As you can expect, some elements of the underground, no pun intended, have tried to conduct their business down here, but our police force are quite vigilant about that kind of problems."

"Then, why are we here?"

"This is where Pete and I meet. I want to show you his last whereabouts. Maybe you can see something that I don't."

Laughing harder, Trip says, "So, *you* are part of the underground conducting business here!"

"No, there is nothing *underground* about what we are doing. It's totally legitimate business!" Simone says as she tries to defend herself.

Wiping a tear from the corner of his eye, it's been a while since Trip has laughed so hard. That certainly brings back memories. While Violet is always bubbly and cheerful, she is not nearly as funny as Simone, who somehow does silly things without recognizing it. He doesn't realize how much he has missed Simone until this very moment. Like Violet, she has the natural ability to make him forget that he is in gloomy and smelly places without ever trying.

Trip says, "OK, OK. I am sorry. Please show me this place."

Still steaming with egg on her face, she tries to sound very serious as she says, "There is another reason that I brought you down here. I want you to see everything we have to offer first so you can make an informed decision."

"Duly noted," Trip says with a serious tone even though he is still laughing on the inside.

*

After walking a short distance, she pretends that all is well again and says, "Here we are. See anything?"

It's a very small office next to a construction site. It's not much, just a break room of some kind. Going in, he is surprised that it actually smells a little better as the scent of fresh coffee and donuts seem to have overpowered the stench outside. Looking at the furnishing, it looks very generic and can belong to anyone at any site. It's a little

61

messy with a few stains on the table and sticky residue around the coffee pot, but that is to be expected.

"Everything looks exactly the way it should," Trip says casually as he continues to scan the items. "Instead of just seeing the place, can you tell me a little bit more about your last meeting with him?"

"Like usual, we come down here separately. He's usually here before I am," Simone says. Pointing towards a lounger, she continues, "He sat over there, as usual, to wait for me. When I got here, he told me that he has seen the stranger that Drew has been meeting. This time, he was able to get close enough to see that this person had blond hair and blue eyes."

"Does he recognize this man?"

"Well, it may not be a man at all. He thinks it may be a woman. Even though couldn't hear the content of the conversation, he thinks it is a woman trying to deepen her voice in disguise."

"Does he have any more descriptions? Is she tall, thin, short, fat, oval face, round face? Anything like that?"

"Nothing specific. I believe he said that she was a little shorter than Drew and wore a completely black outfit with a cape, hood, scarf, gloves, and boots, covering just about everything besides the eyes and parts of her hair. So, it's difficult to see any other discernable details."

"Of course."

Looking at Trip's black outfit, Simone smiles and says, "Perhaps, you two shop from the same store."

"Haha."

"Come to think of it, perhaps you do. As I mentioned before, I believe this mystery person is from Balavan." Simone says as she studies his clothing.

Not sure how to take her comment, Trip tries to brush it off and says, "This is generic garb. It can be from anywhere. I am sure there are seamstresses that can make something like this right here, too."

"That is true."

"Did he not take a photograph or something? In his line of work, you would think that would be the first thing he does. Word of mouth usually does not hold up in court without some hard evidence."

"That may be true, but I didn't hire him to prove anything in *court*. In fact, it's quite the opposite. I don't want to leave any trails, which can be used against me."

"If you don't get any physical proof, how do you know he is telling the truth?" Trip asks.

"Because I have used him before and he has proven himself to be trustworthy."

"How do you know it wasn't all just a show to gain your trust?"

"Wow, I thought we are the paranoid ones. You sound just like one of us!"

"Well, there is a time and place. I think, in this case, there is a valid reason to be suspicious. Where did you find him?"

"At the police station."

"You figure if he is already working on a case, he must be legitimate?"

"That's part of it. I also watched him work to make sure that he knows what he is doing. I find it the best way to gauge a person's abilities. From what I have seen, I am convinced that he is an honest and hardworking man."

"If you were able to get close enough to do that while he was on a case, don't you think he is not very good at his job? I mean a good private investigator would be discreet and know his surroundings."

Gritting her teeth, Simone is a little insulted as she says, "What are you trying to say? That it was all an act and that he suckered me into hiring him?"

"I wouldn't use the word suckered, but yes. I think there is a possibility that you were taken for a ride. The question is: what is he after? Did anything particular happen around the time that he disappeared? Did he take any information from you that may be of use to an enemy?"

"No and definitely no. Nothing happened out of the ordinary around here. Drew makes sure of it. And, I am always careful not to reveal anything confidential to anyone."

Knowing that he has angered her, Trip says, "I am sorry if I have offended you. I am just trying to get a better understanding of what is going on. Do you want to take a break before we continue?"

Now that he has apologized, Simone cannot possibly stay mad at him anymore, at least not outwardly.

"No, I am the one who should apologize."

After a short pause, he smiles and says, "I know you are not going to like it, but I have to ask. How does he manage to meet you down here since every entrance requires an identification scanner?"

"I got him a job as a construction worker. That's his front."

"What type?"

"Does it matter? He doesn't actually work there. In fact, nobody even knows that he exists down here. He only exists on the computer. I made sure I hid all information related to him as deep into the system as I can to avoid any suspicion. I also used fake photographs and addresses so no one knows what he really looks like."

"Even so, I am curious as to what kind of things can he get his hands on? I would think there are certain areas of the construction site that every worker can access. Otherwise, it wouldn't be believable that he is an actual worker, right?"

"Yes, I suppose you are right. I didn't deliberately remove any access."

"So, what is it?" Trip asks again.

"He asked to work on aircrafts."

"You didn't find that suspicious?"

"Frankly, no. He has said that he has always had a fondness of airplanes as a child. So, I didn't see any harm in it."

"Is there a new one being developed right now?"

"We are always developing things down here. I am sure there is."

"Hm," Trip says to himself as he makes a mental note before saying, "Shall we see his house, then?"

Nodding, Simone takes him back to the living area of Algoma through another elevator. Even though she is not happy with his insinuations, she knows that he is right. She has been too careless. She really doesn't know anything about this Pete besides what he has allowed her to know. All of this time, she has been watching her own husband like a hawk thinking that he is the one behind all of the secrets. For the first time in her life, she is second guessing herself.

*

As soon as they arrive, Simone takes out a key to unlock the door.

"He gave you a key to his house?" Trip asks.

"No, but when he disappeared, I picked the lock and made one for myself."

Laughing inside, Trip finds it interesting that there is never a dull minute with her. One moment, he thinks she is a gullible airhead. The next, she is quite crafty and dangerous. There are also times when she does both – like right now. Even though she knows her way around a lock, she does not without putting on a pair of gloves. If he were to enter someone else's home without being invited, he would certainly put one on. For her to ignore something like that, it seems she has done this many times before without even second thinking. Or, perhaps, because she is a town elder, no one ever accuses her of any wrongdoing even if she does get her prints everywhere.

Considering that he is an outsider, he opts to be on the safe side and puts on a pair of black one before saying, "So, there is no sign of forced entry? Did you dust for finger prints and that sort of detective work?"

Following suit, Simone takes out a pair of tan ones and says, "Of course. What do you take me for?"

It's pretty obvious that she is new at this. Despite her position as a co-leader of the Elders, her job doesn't seem to involve a great deal of hand-on field work. That can be another reason she needs help. At least, she is a quick learner.

"Sorry. I am just trying to cover all bases, like I have been all day," Trip says it in a gentle voice, as if he is trying to explain why he was being so brutally honest in interrogating her earlier about Pete without actually saying it.

Smiling, Simone gets the message and says, "I know."

Without saying another word, somehow, they both seem to understand one another a little better after that. With that, they get serious and begin to go from room to room slowly, looking for clues. Within minutes, Trip already finds something of interest – cameras, lots of them. It seems there is a pinhole camera in every room. In some places, there are several of them in different angles.

Pretending not to notice, he continues his inspection. Everything is exactly as Simone has described it, clean, but lived in. It definitely has been staged. There is nothing that says anything. Magazines are neatly piled on the coffee table. Books are put away nicely on the shelves. Looking at the covers, they are all very generic titles that any man would read. There is nothing circled or stained to show anything out of the ordinary and no ear mark of any kind. In fact, many of them look like they have never been read. There are also no pictures of any kind. All of the walls are bare except for a couple of landscaping paintings.

Looking in the closet, it seems Pete has not packed anything. The underwear is stacked in a clean pile. There are no clothes out of the hangers and no holes of any kind to indicate that anything is missing. The same is true of the bathroom. The toothbrush, toothpaste, soap, shampoo, and shaver are all still there – albeit extremely clean, as if they are all brand new. There is not a single water spot or hair in the sink. Taking some baby powder that he has found in the medicine cabinet, he lightly dusts the surfaces. There is not one in sight. While he has expected someone to have cleaned the place if this Pete was captured or has fled, he is surprised not to see *Simone's* fingerprints somewhere.

"I have seen enough. Let's go," Trip says after cleaning up traces of the baby powder.

"Already?" Simone is both excited and confused.

She hasn't found anything out of the ordinary, but is impressed that he has.

After leaving the house, she says, "Well? What have you found?"

"Did you wear gloves last time you went into that house?" Trip asks.

Looking sheepish, Simone admits, "No. Did I mess something up?"

"No," Trip says. After a short pause, he asks, "Does the place look exactly the same as the last time you were there?"

"Yes, I think so."

"I am positive you are being watched right now."

"What? Why would you say that?" Simone asks as she looks around with her eyes while trying not to look obvious.

"Someone came and wiped off all of your prints after you came in. The only way someone would do that is if they knew you come in."

"Who would do something like that?"

"Well, I suspect it's your husband Drew. He may have cleaned up the prints to make sure that you are not caught in the middle of something that he is up to. If that is the case, it means two things. First, your husband still cares about you. Second, Pete is dead. I take it you don't have a photograph of Pete, either."

Shaking her head, Simone cannot believe what she is hearing. Did she lead Pete to his death? If she did, is her husband responsible? She cannot decide which question is more terrifying.

"We need to get you to a safe place."

"No, I can take care of myself. I need to stay exactly where I am. Otherwise, how can I call myself a leader? Besides, I cannot leave my children."

Chapter 6: The Benefactor

Back in Balavan, a prominent figure remains on the scene, albeit in the shadows – Amelia Richardson. Being a well-respected socialite her entire life, she has always had a great deal of time in her hands as she looks for causes to support. When Victor was the Generalissimo, everyone wanted to be a part of her charitable works. After all, she is practically the most famous star in the entire dominion. Who doesn't want to be seen with a celebrity?

If she was into orphans, everyone wanted to help foster homes. When she was on a war path against the Desiderios, the Balavians flocked to buy war bonds. When she was into schools, there were more teachers than ever before. Although she has fallen from grace following Victor's defeat, it is not all bad news. If anyone knows how to make lemonade out of lemons, it's Amelia. For one thing, she still has the power to pull her favors as well as the funds to make things happen. Now that she is no longer being followed everywhere she goes, she can make things happen a lot quicker. It's also a lot easier for her to support a cause that she wishes to keep quiet, like rebuilding Algoma.

Even though Amelia pretends that she stays out of her husband's business, she is more involved than she wants the rest of the world to believe, including her own husband. Without asking directly, she uses Victor's journals to find out what towns the Legionnaires have sacked and why. While she is no saint by any stretch of the imagination, she does feel like she wants to make amend for people she truly believes have been wronged. In some cases, it is even clear to Victor that he and his men have gone too far as evidenced in the following entry.

*

August 27, 2068

This is getting out of hand. My men are becoming ruthless. Even though they still fear me, they will do almost anything if I do not specifically forbid them from doing so. This morning, I saw them kill a child for no reason at all. Even in times of war, there should be rules that are given. What is wrong with them? I really wanted to go over there and strangle him with my bare hands, but I didn't. I wish I did, though. It would have taught those renegades a thing or two about moral conscience, which they obviously do not have.

*

This was the day that the Legionnaires sacked Algoma, Trip's homeland. Amelia remembers this day well. It was the day that Victor came home in complete silence with a very irritated looking expression on his face. He refused to say a word until she begged him. Then, he recounted everything that he saw on the battlefield. He was utterly disgusted by what he saw his own men did, but he didn't do anything to stop them. Why? Why would he be so angry but just stand by and watch as they destroy innocent people? It was almost as if he had lost his own humanity on that day since he knew that ultimately he was responsible for their actions. It was too late.

She also remembered the days after the battle. She had felt so bad for the Algomians that she paid them a visit the next day. Trying to stay incognito, she went there alone and in disguise. She also made sure that she was far enough away that no one could recognize her. Using her binoculars, she could see the burned bodies and the starving and filthy children who had been crying over their parents. It was a sight she could never forget and she never did.

Over the next few years, she had been secretly paying them a visit in disguise, helping them whenever, wherever, and however she could. She would always be dressed in black, covering everything from head to toe. The only visible part of her are her eyes and her hands. Whenever someone would ask her name, she would also reply, call me "Mom". She is also the mystery donor who has been giving them the money to rebuild their tribe. Only one person knows her true identify – Drew. He was the young boy she first saw on that fateful day, crying over his mother's corpse. Because she lost her biological child, she was more than eager to take him in as her own.

Trying to keep it a secret from everyone, including her husband, however, she had sent three of her servants, Miranda, Karina, and Adriana, to look after him and the other children, rotating days to minimize any suspicion. Because they are always dressed exactly like Amelia, donning a blond wig and colored contacts to match her eyes exactly, the children never realized that they were actually four different people. They had called each one of them "Mom." Hence, without actually bringing him back to Balavan, she watched over him and made sure that he was alright. In time, Drew actually thought of her as his real mother.

It's ironic, really. Drew's new mother is married to the man who is responsible for killing his real one. Till this day, she still visits the area to make sure that everything is doing well. Because she did not specify how they are to use the money, however, she is a little baffled by the amount of security that he has installed in his homeland. Even though she thinks it's an overkill, she is not about to tell him how to run his tribe.

71

Victor had always known that she was up to something, but he did not ask what. All he knew was that whatever she was doing was making her happy. He had not seen her this cheerful since her pregnancy, which was a subject that they both avoided at all cost since that fateful day.

Since the death of their first born, it was like this for them. Unless it was so terrible that they knew it was killing the other person, they would stay out of each other's business unless the information was volunteered. At that point, then, they would offer their assistance anyway they could, because they knew that it must be important enough for them to share.

Right now, Amelia is wondering how Drew is holding up. When she thinks about him, a smile comes on her face. He is like a son to her. After losing a biological child at birth and having an adopted one turn on her, she is in desperate need of another one who can give her the unconditional love she has always craved. Even though she has no official relationship with him, she is more proud of him than she is of Thom right now. Who can blame her?

Unlike Thom who often challenges her almost at every turn, Drew has never contradicted her. It was probably Victor's fault for doting Thom so. Being his only legitimate heir, Victor had given him the world, which makes his betrayal that much more painful. Why is she still thinking about that ungrateful boy? That is all water under the bridge now. She needs to focus more on brighter things. Drew certainly fits the bill.

As far as she is concerned, Drew has not failed her yet. If it wasn't for him, she would have no one to lean on anymore. Even though she is a very independent woman, there are days when she just needs an understanding shoulder to lie on. After the recent events, she is very happy to still have Drew by her side, at least in spirit if not in person. Otherwise, she would no longer have a reason to live. The last time she saw him, he seemed to be doing well. He had heard that the Legionnaires who had destroyed his home had been defeated and was happy about that. It kills her not to be able to tell him about Victor.

*

As she is thinking about him, her maid comes in and says, "I am sorry to interrupt, but there is a gentleman here to see you."

Looking at the clock, she says, "Now? It's already midnight. Who is it?"

"He says his name is Pete and that it is urgent."

Upon hearing the name, she says, "Bring him in! Bring him in!"

Straightening herself up, Amelia gets up to the door and rushes to meet him, "Hello, darling! How is everything?"

"Everything is just as planned," Pete says.

"Are you hungry?" Amelia asks before shouting, "Miranda, can you give us a couple of turkey sandwiches and a couple of beers?"

Smiling, Pete says, "Ah, my favorites!"

"Certainly! Nothing but the best for you!" Amelia says with a chuckle.

Patting the sofa, she says, "Come, sit, sit. Tell me everything!"

"As you expected, our boy is building everything according to specifications."

"So, when can we be ready?"

"Well, even though the weapons are ready, we still have a few loose ends."

"Oh, you mean that little wench Simone?"

"Yes," Pete says as he nods.

"What has she done now? She didn't find out who you really are, did she?"

"No, of course not. She still thinks Pete is a code name," Pete says as he laughs.

"So, why do you think she may cause a problem?"

"She has been snooping around too much. I had to disappear a few weeks ago because she got too close."

"How so?"

"She started inspecting the testing area and asking questions. I didn't want to let her see me there."

"How do you plan on explaining your disappearance?"

"I haven't thought that far yet. I figure I will let her imagination run wild for a while and see where it takes her. Usually, that works pretty well. She is so suspicious of her husband now that she can blame him for all sorts of things."

"You really shouldn't do that. That poor boy," Amelia says.

"Well, he insists. He is willing to do anything for you, you know that."

"That doesn't mean you should make it harder for him than necessary," Amelia lectures.

"I know, I know. I apologize. I will think of something."

"So, tell me. How is your little cat and mouse game with little Miss Nosey?"

"I got her all revved up about a mysterious woman dressed in black that Drew is meeting," Pete says as he laughs. "I think she thinks her husband is having an affair. Isn't that great?"

"Do you really think she will fall for something like that?"

"So far, she seems quite gullible. She has been in a bubble for so long. I don't think she knows what to think. All she knows is that Drew is behind everything. And, Drew has been a champ, doing his part to confuse her thoroughly. By making her think that she is the real power behind the group, she thinks nothing goes on there without her approval, which means she will not pay too much attention to things that we are doing.

By alienating her physically, it makes her think that something is wrong with their marriage, which makes her focus her attention on him. If she keeps tailing him instead of me, we can launch this thing quickly."

"It sounds like a pretty good plan."

"But..."

"Of course there is a but. What's going on?"

"As I was leaving, I heard that El Diablo was in town."

"What? That is going to ruin everything! We have to get rid of him. Why didn't you say so earlier?"

"Yes, that's why I am here."

"You couldn't have just picked up the phone and told me?"

"You know all phone communications are monitored in that place. I cannot risk it."

"So, what do you think we should do?"

"Obviously, we need to get rid of El Diablo before he gets a wind of what is going on."

"And, how do you suppose we get rid of the Demon himself? I heard he cannot die."

"Oh, come on. It's just an overinflated image. He's human, like everyone else."

"Even so, there must be a reason why he has such a reputation. It cannot just be pure luck. He was shot three times in the chest and acted like nothing happened. We need to find his secret."

"OK. I can take that on. That sounds like a nice challenge. What do you want to do with little Miss Nosey?" Pete asks.

"For Drew's sake, I hope she doesn't do anything stupid. I would have to have to take care of her, too. It would break his heart."

"OK, I will leave her alone for now. I will let you know when she crosses that line before I do anything *permanent.*"

"Good. It's settled, then. Let's enjoy our little snack, shall we?"

*

Unbeknownst to Simone, Pete has been working for Amelia from the very beginning. After Amelia came to Algoma to help the children 23 years ago, she knew she needed help to rebuild the tribe. She obviously couldn't get it from Victor since he was the one who destroyed the tribe to begin with. It also rules out everyone else related to the Legionnaires. At the time, that included a large portion of Balavan. At the same time, she could not trust anyone who might have been affiliated with enemies of the Legionnaires either.

Despite her vast disposable income and her ability to raise funds for charities, money does nothing in the hands of children who do not know how to use it properly. Initially, the only thing she could do was create makeshift hospitals staffed by her own maids and tents used as soup kitchen filled from her own pantries in order to save the children. Before long, Amelia knew that it was time for something more substantial. After some extensive searching, she finally found Pete, an independent contractor who had no allegiance to anyone, which was certainly a very rare trait to help the rebuilding process.

Being an orphan himself, he had always been a loner. Even at a young age, he knew that people can be cruel, sometimes for no reason at all. As such, he never cared about how he looked or what people said or thought about him. While he always wears clean clothes, they are usually outdated and show signs of wear. That's how he likes them. In his mind, wear and tear equates to comfort. Why wear things that only look fashionable but are uncomfortable? That is just a way of torturing yourself for the sake of vanity. He also does not like to cut his wavy brown hair or shave his beard. While he always washes and trims them, he lets his hair down like a hippie.

Hence, it's little surprise that the way he dresses leads some to see him as nothing more than a drifter who does odd jobs that come by. Because he lives a simple life, he does not need much. When he does have work, he rents a place to live. When he does not, he can easily live off of the land. Unlike most people, he enjoys the great outdoors, which makes him more like Trip than he realizes. It gives him a sense of freedom and tranquility that he cannot find anywhere else. While a nice hot bath is much appreciated at times, he also enjoys a nice shower under the waterfall.

While he may appear to be nothing more than a common vagabond to some, Amelia sees much more than that. Despite the darkness of his big brown eyes, he has a twinkle in his eyes that speaks volumes about his intelligence. As soon as she first laid eyes on him, she knew he would be a wonderful asset for her grandiose project, even before she knew what he could do for her. It didn't really matter really. She knew that once he's on board, he can learn whatever skills that is necessary. All she has to do is win him over first, which is a lot more difficult than she anticipated.

During their first meeting, it started out as quite a disaster and was kind of pathetic from his point of view. He was sitting on a park bench, taking in the fresh air with his eyes closed as he took in the sun when Amelia approached him and sat down. Although the bench was certainly big enough to accommodate both of them, it was undoubtedly a strange sight. The two of them looked like day and night as they stared at each other awkwardly in silence for a second. Dressed in the latest fashion along with pointy and very uncomfortable heels, she turned to him with a box of donuts and a large carafe of fresh coffee in hand.

Seemingly out of the blue, she said, "Would you like to have some? They are freshly made less than fifteen minutes ago."

Thinking that she has mistaken him for a homeless man, he politely said, "No thanks," as he returned to minding his own business.

Yet, she was not deterred as she kept pushing it to him.

"Are you sure? Mmmmm, it's delicious," she said as she took the tiniest of bites in one of the honey glazed treats while making an obvious sipping sound as she took a small drink out of the coffee.

"I am sure," he confirmed.

Nevertheless, she repeated the offer several times using different words. Ironically, it had the opposite effect than she hoped as she started to become impatient, making her sound more condescending with each word. Not knowing how to interact with someone like him, Amelia made him feel like a pathetic child who can be won by sweets, or worse, a charity case who can be tempted easily by cheap theatrics. Despite his appearance, he is a very proud man who has never accepted handouts. Besides, the way she insisted came off pushy, as if she were one of those high society snobs who feel like it is their duty to give to the poor only so they can brag about it to their peers. Her persistence was getting on his last nerve. When he got up to leave, she made things even worse by patronizing him with insincere apologies.

"Oh, I am so sorry. Please do not go. I do not mean to offend you," she had said putting her hand on her chest.

Although she spoke the correct words, the tone was exaggerated and body language clearly forced. It's a mystery as to why he ever turned back to listen to her at all. While every fiber of his being told him to walk away from this crazy woman, a part of him told him that he should hear her out. He did not know why. It might be because he thought she had a desperate look in her eyes or because the encounter was so unusual. In either case, after what seemed like the most painful few minutes of awkward conversation, she finally told him that she intended on hiring him for a major project for starving children that will be quite profitable for him.

Who can possibly turn down an offer that helps poor youths and make money at the same time? Opportunities like this are definitely rare. Although he had his suspicions about the authenticity of the offer, he figures he has nothing to lose. What can she possibly take from him that can be of any worth to her? He has no material possessions or connections to speak of. If anything else, she stands to have a lot more to lose than he does.

After careful consideration, Pete agrees to join her team, but only on his own terms. It's like a builder's dream. He is able to dress any way he liked, do as he wanted, and given the money to spend as he wished. If he wanted to build himself a mansion first, he could. If he wanted to have lobster for dinner, he didn't even need to ask. All he had to do was charge it to her name. In addition, he could build the new town according to his own designs and schedule. It's rare for Amelia to put so much trust in any one person, but, for some reason, she did with Pete – and still does. She only has two conditions.

First, he is to keep this between the two of them. No one else must know of the plan. If he needs to hire workers, he will have to use whatever resource they already have. If he must recruit from outside, they must be given a cover story that is so convincing that they would have no reason to suspect otherwise. Second, he is welcome to come and go as he wishes, but he is not to show up at her house when her husband is around. When she first gave him that condition, he smiled, thinking that she was just a bored housewife trying to spend her husband's money without his knowledge. To him, it makes her human. She was no longer just money bags to him.

Of course, as soon as he found out that she was married to Victor, he nearly negated on their agreement. Even though he was not impacted by Victor's actions in Algoma personally, he just didn't feel right. It was as if he himself was being a hypocrite. It wasn't until Amelia presented him with Victor's journal entries showing that he was not the monster he thought he was that Pete reluctantly agreed to continue their arrangement. Although it was no excuse, at least, he understood. This was the moment that Amelia knew that she had made the right choice. He was the perfect person for the job. He had principle, yet was emotionless to the untrained eye.

When he first saw the children of Algoma, any hesitation he may have had completely disappeared. His initial reaction was heartbreak. It was difficult to watch so many helpless children. He would have helped them for free if he had the means. Like Amelia, he chose to have a specific look when he visited them. As soon as they saw a shaggy looking man wearing a red baseball cap, aviator sunglasses, blue t-shirt, torn blue jeans, and white sneakers, they knew it was him. Like her, he became known as "Dad" to them. None of the children ever knew either one of their real names.

As the years went by, they have become a real team. They have a strange relationship, one where they are as close to a husband and wife as two people can get without the physical part of the relationship. They knew what each other's thoughts. They could complete one another's sentences. And, they would bend over backwards to give the other what they wanted even if they themselves did not agree. This latest project is a good example. When she told him her desire to get Algoma ready for war, he did not stand in her way because he knew it was important to her. When the time comes, she will tell him. For now, she has kept the reason to herself. Nevertheless, he has a feeling that he already knows the answer – to avenge her husband against the evil demon. Despite his personal feelings towards Victor, Pete knows that this is something he wants to do for her in order to give her some peace.

As the children became young adults, both he and Amelia have started to keep their distance from them. Hence, even though they have both seen Simone grow up with Drew, neither youngster remembers either one of their faces. As designed, the children identified them more with their general appearance than their actual faces. As long as they do not wear the exact same ensemble and wear their hair as they did before, none of the children would know who they are. Simone's reaction to Pete is a perfect

81

example. Even though she has a good feeling about working with the man, she has no idea who he really is.

That is one reason why he made sure his house in Algoma is completely vanilla, devoid of any identifiable characteristic. By keeping nothing personal around, it makes it more difficult for any of them to make the connection. How can they? When they think of "Mom" and "Dad", they think of a parent who would have pictures of all of their children everywhere to remind them of a loving family.

In order to make sure that he leaves nothing behind when he is not there, he makes a point of wiping everything down before leaving his house, which is why Trip cannot find any prints of any kind when he went into Pete's house. As for the pinhole cameras, they are all fake, except for one on the front door, which is so small and discrete that no one else knows it's there. It is also one of his own designs, which only he can access. If anyone else attempts to view it, it will dissolve instantly, leaving no trace of its existence. In addition, it is motion censored and only goes off when someone besides him has entered the house. Then, as he gets within ten feet of the door upon his return, it would notify him and only him if it has triggered and whether or not the intruder is still inside.

The rest of the cameras are nothing buy dummy props to throw people like Trip away, much like the way some people have dummy security cameras outside of their houses. By having so many of them, it makes it more difficult to find the real one. By having them around the house, its scares the common intruders away as they certainly do not want to stay long enough to be caught. It also deters them from ever returning again. A nice comfortable house like this is very likely to attract squatters when he is away. Finally, by not making them readily noticeable, they are much more believable.

At the same time, people like Simone would not suspect him because they think they have him under complete surveillance at all times when the exact opposite is true. With Drew on his side, he has a recorded footage of him doing regular day to day things in the different parts of the house on hand, just in case suspicion does arise. With no time stamp on the original recordings, they can be altered to include one at any time whenever necessary. So far, it has been a perfect setup.

Chapter 7: Back from the Dead

With his new mission at hand, Pete goes back to Algoma as if nothing has happened. As soon as he returns to his house, he knows someone has been there. He has expected as much. He has never been away from Algoma for so long without someone breaking in, usually a member of the Elders like Drew or Simone who wonders where he has gone or bored children who just want to have a place to party and have fun.

Taking out a pendant on his neck, he clicks on a button and instantly a hologram image is displayed showing him the footage of Simone and Trip entering his home. This is the first time he has seen El Diablo in action, sort of. Like everyone else, he has only heard of him. Like everyone else, he is surprised at how normal he looks. As he watches, he studies his demeanor to find out how he walks and carries himself. While he is impressed with his poise and smoothness, he has not seen anything that shouts: invincibility – not that he expected to. It would be too easy.

Now, he has to figure out where they have gone. Although he is disappointed that the footage does not give him a clue, he is not surprised. If Trip had given a hint, it would have been a trap or a test anyways. After all, why would someone as cunning as the Demon himself be so careless? He certainly couldn't have lived so long if he were. Being married to Drew, Simone would not dare to bring Trip to her home or anywhere else near him. Instead, she would try to put him somewhere with as little surveillance as possible – the testing area. That will be his first stop.

While Simone has a set of secured elevators and passageways, Pete has a completely different set of them. Of course, unlike hers, his are completely hidden and accessible only by him. No one knows their existence, not Drew, and not even Amelia. Being the architect of the town definitely has its benefits. Instead of putting them in the most obscure places, he puts them in the most obvious places. One of which is almost too cliché - in his own closet behind his clothes.

There is no need to scan his palm. It's like an automatic door. If he is the only one in the house, it opens spontaneously when he gets within a foot of it. It opens up in a bathroom of an old nearly finished house in the testing area. From the outside, it looks like an older model home that no one wants, but it's in a relatively good shape that no one would think to demolish it, either. On the inside, it has a state of the art monitoring system.

Before getting out, Pete scans the house for any disturbances. He figures if Trip is hiding in this region, he will most probably pick one of the ones that are almost complete. When he is sure that no one else is there, he steps out which also activates his security system. Now, he can comfortably scan the rest of the testing area without interruption. As he looks at the construction area, he is satisfied that the engineers and the rest of the crew are hard at work. He sees lots of familiar faces even if he does not remember their names. He double backs a few times when he sees people who he does not immediately recognize. After scrutinizing them, he is satisfied that they belong there. Then, he sees a familiar face that does not belong in the construction site – Simone.

Smiling, he wonders what little Miss Nosey is doing building aircrafts. As far as he knows, she knows next to nothing about the manufacturing or the designing of a plane. In fact, she seems to have distaste for that sort of thing and prefers to stay away from it. Nevertheless, he is impressed that she blends in so well with everyone else. He wonders if anyone else knows who she is or just thinks that she is a new recruit or trainee. Judging from the fact that she is not shadowing anyone, it's safe to say that she has convinced them that she is skilled. If Simone is there, there is a good chance Trip may be. She is obviously there for a good reason.

Zooming in closer, he looks to see if he can find the mysterious El Diablo. After going over the area several times, he is satisfied that the Demon is not there. Perhaps, he is hiding somewhere and using Simone as bait. If that is the case, he must be somewhere high and hidden. Looking at the ventilation systems on top, he turns on the infrared to see if there are any human beings in there, but finds none. Then, he turns his attention to all of the smoke filled areas that can be used as cover, which is actually a more difficult task than it appears. There are simply too many people congregating in those areas to take a cigarette break or just to chat. It's difficult to discern their faces in the mists. There is a definite possibility that Trip may be hiding in one of those places.

"Well, two can play this game," Pete says to himself.

Wearing his well-worn construction uniform, he goes to the hazy areas of the site to smoke a fake cigarette. As he leans against the wall, he is listening to the others talk and watching them quietly without drawing any attention.

"Hey, man, how's it going?" a man wearing the same uniform as he does comes up and leans against the wall next to him as he lights up a cigarette.

"Hey," Pete replies, trying to ignore him.

"Have you heard that we have a new visitor?" the man asks.

"Who?" Pete says, pretending to be curious.

"The famous El Diablo, of course!"

"Oh, yeah, I heard," he replies casually.

"So, what do you think?"

"What is there to think about? It's none of my business."

"What do you mean? A famous guy like that? Out of the blue? Don't you think it's cool?"

"Sure, I guess."

"Well, I think it is. I wonder what he is doing here."

"Beats me."

"I heard that he is coming to take over the down and overthrow our illustrious leader."

"Why would he do that?"

"I hear that he and Drew are romantic rivals."

Snickering, Pete is actually surprised by this latest rumor. All of this time he is trying to get Simone to think that Drew has a mistress on the side, word around town seems to imply that she is the cheater. This is almost too funny.

"Why would they say that?"

"Don't you know? They were all friends when they were little. Drew could never get her attention back then. He had to pretend to be his friend so he could get close to her. Isn't that pathetic?" the man says as he laughs.

At least, the gossip mill is in full session. While this may sound like a harmless sly against their Elder, it can be much more dangerous. It seems Trip's arrival may be tarnishing Drew's reputation. Even if it's not against his abilities, a damaged image can make things much more difficult for him and Amelia to carry out their plan. It's best to do some damage control before things get out of hand.

"Oh, come on. They were all kids back then. You can hardly label him pathetic over something you think they did when they were in grade school. Besides, from what I hear,

Simone and Drew's marriage are solid. They have two beautiful children, didn't they?"

"Yeah, I guess, but what if this Diablo is back to reclaim his woman? Wouldn't that be something?"

"Reclaim?" Pete doesn't like the use of that word.

It's obvious that this man also has little respect for Simone if he thinks she is a mere property to be *reclaimed.* Even if he does not have as great of a respect for her as he should, she is not some object to be passed around between two men. If she were to hear him say that, she would most definitely give him a good shiner.

"Why would he do that? Doesn't the great El Diablo have the Warrior already? There is no reason for him to break up a marriage."

"Hey I am only saying what I heard. Sounds like you are defending this fellow. Do you know him or something?"

That's not good. He has said too much, or at least, the wrong things. He needs to do something before this man start to get suspicious or nosey.

Acting aloof, he looks uninterested and says, "No. Just by reputation."

This is one of those times when less is definitely more. By looking like he could care less, this man will most likely drop it and he is right.

"Anyways, so what are you working on?" the man says, changing the subject.

Even though, once again, he is just making conversation, he has started a topic that Pete wants to avoid. While he knows every project that is going on in the entire town, he does not want to give the man too much details in case if he a part of the same project. That way, he can have deniability later if someone recognizes him elsewhere.

"Come on, you know it's confidential. I am going to have to kill you if I tell you," Pete says jokingly.

"Yes, yes. Never mind that I asked," the man says with a laugh.

That was a close one, but apparently, he did a good job.

With that, the man says, "Oh, well, time to get back to work. Later."

"Later."

*

Not wanting to attract further undue attention, Pete decides to head inside to find Simone and continue their little charade instead of risking another uncomfortable encounter.

"Hello," he says as he passes by.

"Hey, you! Thank goodness, you are OK! Thought you disappeared from the face of the earth. Where have you been?" Simone whispers in surprise.

Not knowing his connection with Amelia, she is excited to know that Pete has not died like Trip thought. As far as she is concerned, this is excellent news. Now, he can help them figure out what Drew is up to – at least so she thinks.

"Not here," Pete says as he walks out.

She knows exactly what that means. Pretending to be finishing up whatever it was she was doing with the wing, she cleans her hands and casually walks about a few minutes later.

Going to the break room, she gives him a hug and says, "It's so good to see you. How have you been?"

"Good."

"Where have you been all of this time? I feared the worst when I didn't hear from you for so long."

"I apologize. I hope you didn't worry too much. I followed our mysterious guest and just got back and didn't have the time to tell you where I'd gone."

Surprised to hear it, Simone says, "And? What did you find out?"

"It appears that she is from Balavan," Pete says.

"Who is she?"

"Just some teacher."

Looking a little confused, she asks, "Why would he need to meet secretly with an ordinary teacher from Balavan?"

Making the story up as he goes, he says, "She came to the area to conduct research on surrounding lands a few months ago, but didn't come close enough to trigger the perimeter alarms."

"Then, how did he know she was there?" Simone wonders.

"He was on the surface, surveying the area to see if there are any holes in the security when he spotted her."

Nodding, Simone seems to believe his explanation, but asks, "Why hasn't he talked about her?"

"You know how he is. In exchange for her not talking about Balavan to her peers, he has agreed to keep her activities quiet."

"That makes sense," Simone says, but asks, "So, why is he still talking with her?"

"He isn't. She concluded her research three weeks ago and went home. I followed her just to be sure of it."

Nodding, Simone says, "So, I have nothing to worry about then." After a short pause, she continues, "Why did she need to meet him at such odd hours?"

"That is by Drew's request. He wants to keep everything between the two of them so no one would ask any questions."

Even though Pete has been able to answer all of her questions, it's obvious that she is not fully convinced that her husband is not conducting any shady activities, personal or not.

"Still, I want to know about her – just in case."

Figuring that she is not going to go all the way to Balavan to check this cover story, Pete decides to use one of Amelia's clones as the basis behind this mystery woman. He just has to be careful to give only enough details to satisfy her curiosity without arousing suspicion.

"Let's see. Her name is Adriana. She is in her early 40's, lives alone. She is a botanist who teaches Biology at the new University in Balavan. With the end of the Six Year War, the school decided that they wanted to know more about local habitats. So, she volunteered to survey plants around neighboring villages."

"Hm," Simone says as she looks like she is in deep thought.

Trying to get her to not overthink it, he changes the conversation and says, "On my way back, I heard that El Diablo has graced us with his presence. Is that right?"

Just as Pete has expected, Simone instantly looks happier as she says, "Yes, he is."

"Is he still in town?"

"Yes."

"I would be remiss if I don't meet this legend!"

"Oh, he is not the meet and greet kind. He's kind of quiet."

"That's too bad! But, hey, I guess that makes him fit right in here, doesn't he?" Pete says jokingly.

"Yes, yes it does."

Realizing that she has no intention of revealing Trip's location, Pete decides not to waste any more time.

"Well, since we have concluded our business with the mystery woman, I guess I will be on my way. You can drop off your payment at my house anytime," Pete says casually.

"Will do. Thanks for everything," Simone says, seemingly oblivious of his true intentions.

*

As he takes his leave, he does not get far as he waits for her to lead him to Trip from his secret surveillance building. Now that he has told her about his return, it will not seem as suspicious if she happens to see him in the area later. Yet, he cannot be too open because he is not supposed to be a real engineer, as far as she is concerned. After watching her for the next hour, however, he has not gotten any closer to finding Trip. Instead, Simone seems to be more interested in the stockpile of weapons than anything else. Even when most of the workers have gone home, she is still there.

Just as he is about to give up for the day, he sees her leave the area and heading towards her private elevator. It seems it's finally time for her to call it quits, too. At that moment, Pete's stomach starts to growl. Looking at the time, he realizes it is already 8PM. Where has the time gone? Expecting her to go back home to Drew and her children, Pete is getting up to shut down his system and head back up to his house. Just then, he notices the elevator coming back down.

"That's strange. There is no one calling it from down here. Has she forgotten something?" he wonders.

Turning on the infrared light in the elevator, he smiles. There are two people in the elevator. As soon as the door opens, he sees that she has returned with the illusive visitor – El Diablo. Apparently, she is simply waiting for the coast to be clear before bringing him back down for private investigating. Turning up the volume, Pete is hoping to be able to eavesdrop on their conversation. He is glad that everyone else has left for the day. Otherwise, there would be too much interference to hear them clearly.

"How was your day?" Simone asks.

"Good," Trip answers in his usual short and concise non-answer.

"Well, I thought you might be interested to know that my Private Investigator showed up out of the blue today. He's not dead after all! Isn't that great"

Pete is smiling as he listens to Simone's excitement. He is quietly congratulating himself for having done a great job with his little performance earlier.

"Really?"

"Yes, he said he was following the mystery woman for the past three weeks and found that she was nothing more than a research botanist who works at a University in Balavan."

Being a plant enthusiast, he says, "What was her name?"

"Some woman named Adriana."

As Simone recounts her conversation with Pete, Trip listens with a concerned look on his face.

Finally, he says, "I don't believe him."

"Uh, oh," Pete mumbles. He knows it's too good to be true. Someone as skilled as Trip can always sniff out trouble.

"I was afraid you were going to say that. I was wondering if he was telling the truth or not, too, but what reason would he have to lie?"

"I don't know. Are you sure this place is secure?" he asks as he looks around.

"Yes, I scoped it out today. There is not a single audio or video device anywhere."

"Then, why do I feel like I am being watched?"

"Well, now that you say it, I feel a chill, too," Simone says.

Rolling his eyes, Pete whispers to himself, "Why is it every time someone says they feel something everyone else has to, too?"

"Come on, let's get out of here," Simone says.

"No, if we are being watched, whoever it is already knows that we are here. So, there is no point hiding it. If it's Drew or any of his men, they would have barged in by now to stop us from seeing whatever it is that he does not want us to see. It's no secret that he doesn't like me. Since I don't hear any footsteps or elevators going up and down, it's safe to say that it is not your loving husband. My guess is whoever is watching us doesn't want us to know. So, he is not going to interrupt or confront us. Besides, you are a member of the Elders. You have every right to be here and I am here as your guest. So, I say we keep doing what we came to do, but do it discretely, like we are just touring the place."

Nodding, Simone says, "Agreed."

After closer examination, Trip sees some disturbing markings on them. Despite efforts to disguise them, he recognizes them anywhere. They look very much like the ones from the Legionnaires. It's an irony that is almost too painful to admit. How can Algoma stockpile weapons from the Legionnaires, the same people who destroyed them in the first place? It's pretty obvious that they have no idea what those markings mean, but there is no mistaking them. He has seen too many of them before during those six long years of war with them. He had thought they have destroyed them all, but apparently, many of them have been smuggled over here to be refitted or repaired.

"What's the matter?" Simone asks when she sees his pale expression.

"Nothing. I have seen enough. Let's go." Trip says.

Simone knows what that means. Quickly, they both leave and return to the surface.

"Well? Can you tell me now?" Simone asks once they are back on top.

"No, not yet," Trip says as he points towards the outside bridge.

Nodding, Simone signals that she understands as she leads them outside of the city.

*

"Ugh," Pete mutters to himself again. Trip is too good at this game. Before his arrival, Pete never had a need to install surveillance equipment outside of Algoma before. Apparently, Trip knows that all too well. Now, Pete will have no idea what they are really saying and has to go outside to investigate in person.

*

Once they are back out in the open air, Simone finally says, "Is this far enough?"

"Yes. What do you know about this Pete?"

"Nothing really, besides what I have already told you."

"If he is a private investigator, he is not working for you. He is the one investigating you."

Surprised, she asks, "Why do you say that?"

"I am pretty sure he is hiding something. That story about Adriana is a lie."

"How do you know?"

"The story doesn't add up. Besides, I have never heard of a botanist in the University by that name."

"I didn't know you were close with the faculty members."

"I frequent their labs and got to know most of them. If there is such a project, it's not sanctioned by the University."

Leaning against the tree, Trip takes out his black bottle and starts drinking from it.

She says, "What is that stuff you drink anyways?"

"It's my dinner. Want some?" Trip says as he extends his arm to offer her a sip.

Looking disgusted, she waves her hand and says, "No, thanks. I am not that hungry."

"Suit yourself," Trip says as he continues to enjoy his meal.

"Anyways, what do you suggest we do now?" Simone asks eagerly.

"There is more."

"It's about the stockpile, isn't it?"

Nodding, Trip tells her about the markings that he found. With each word, Simone's face gets redder. She cannot believe her ears.

"Are you sure?" she finally says as she grips her first.

"Yes," Trip says calmly.

Referring to his theory that Pete may be dead; Simone is in denial and says, "You have been wrong before. Maybe you are wrong this time."

Not liking her implication, Trip says, "You believe what you want. I am just telling you what I think."

"I am sorry. I didn't mean it."

"Don't worry about it. I think you should go home and take care of your children."

Nodding, Simone says, "Yes, you are right. It's getting late. See you in the morning."

With that, Trip is left to rehash the conversation over. It doesn't really matter if she means it or not. He knows that Simone is entirely too gullible for her own good. He himself is convinced that Pete and Drew are in it together to destroy Balavan. What he cannot understand is why Drew would do such a thing. He must know where his stockpile of weapons came from. How can he not?

Then again, he may be just as gullible as his wife and they are both nothing more than puppets being pulled by Pete. The more Trip ponders the possibility, the more certain he is that hometown is preparing to attack his new home. No matter how he sees it, it's a lose-lose situation for him. He needs to stop it before it's too late.

Chapter 8: Battle of the Mind

Just like with Pete, Simone has given Trip a new identity in the system – Devin. She thinks it's quite clever. After all, it means that of the dark haired one and he certainly fits the bill. In addition to being true to actual meaning, she chose it because of its close spelling to his moniker El Diablo, the Devil.

Trip rather likes it. It's catchy, yet common enough in Algoma to not raise much suspicion. Because of the need for additional builders for the munition plant, Drew has been hiring new recruits regularly. It's the perfect place for her to sneak an extra one without raising any flags.

In order to immerse himself in his new disguise, he has rented a home in Algoma as Devin. It's a small, modest home in the middle of town. He figures the best place to hide is in the open. No one will think to look for him there. To create this new persona, he cut his hair and changed the way he dresses. No longer does he wear completely black outfits. Ironically, it attracts too much attention. Because only the mortuary staff wears all black, he stands out in the crowd when there are no funeral concessions. Instead, he opts for a very casual t-shirt and blue jeans, like most of the men in town.

Instead of keeping to himself, like he normally does, he makes a point of being friendly to everyone he sees. Yet, he keeps the conversation to a minimum and keeps the topics to the weather or food. That way, no one thinks that there is a mysterious or suspicious looking stranger amongst them. Although the changes seem small, his transformation is quite drastic. If you don't know him, you would never think he is the same man.

By being the common man, he has a better chance of spying on others without being noticed. If he had been El

Diablo, he wouldn't be able to get out of his front door without people crowding around to watch him. He might as well have a giant sign in front of his face that says "Annoy Me."

Now, as long as he keeps clear of Drew and his clones, he is free to do as he wishes there. Of course, his curiosity is getting the better of him. The first thing he wants to do as an anonymous Algomian is to see Simone as a wife and mother.

Since both she and Drew are Elders, he figures they would live in one of the best homes in town. He is right. After walking around town for about thirty minutes, taking in the sights, he comes across a beautiful chateau. It's bigger than most, but not so big that it stands out from the rest. In addition to the bright colors, there are flowers of every color and style all around it. It's exactly the way that he has imagined Simone's house to look like.

Although Trip dislikes what he is about to do, somehow he cannot stop himself from doing it. He is about to be a peeping tom, for the first time in his life. After finding the perfect bush to use as the lookout place, he can see inside of their house. Like a happy family, it's almost picturesque. The house itself looks very warm and inviting. In the living room, there is a gentle smokeless fire in the fireplace as Brittany and Bryce tackle Drew from two different directions while they giggle happily. There is little doubt that the children love their father and the feeling is quite mutual.

In the kitchen, there are big pots of fresh herbs as Simone smiles at the sound of the laughter while she finishes cleaning the dishes. In the hallway are portraits of the family from different milestones of their lives, including their wedding, birth of their children, and various athletic events. There is nothing that indicates trouble in paradise. There is no look of sadness from anyone. Trip feels almost guilty for staying in Algoma, as if a part of him knows that he is contributing to the breakup of this family even though that is definitely not his intention. Yet, at the same time, he is relieved that Simone seems to be happy with her family life. Now that he has satisfied his curiosity, it is time for him to give them some privacy and focus on the main suspect – Pete.

*

While Trip is trying to find out more about Pete, Pete is trying to do the same to him. Knowing that Trip is not the type of man who likes to be around people, he goes outside of Algoma to look for clues. Without the benefit of the cameras, he has to depend on his senses. Staring at every foot print and touching every piece of fallen branch, he tries to channel a scout. He is glad that this job is not going to be as difficult as he thinks. With few visitors, there are only so many people who may have been lingering in the area in the past few days. In addition, because of the dry terrain, the prints are easily distinguishable in the sand. Although the wind often erases them over time, it just means that any that are still on the ground must be new.

Being the architect of Algoma, he knows that there are only so many ways anyone can come in and out of the underground town. Having shadowed Simone several times before, he knows the best place to start, the warning signs around the bridge. Studying the area, he can see two distinct sets of prints. Although both sets are made by heavy boots.

It's pretty clear that one is made by a petite woman and the other by a man. Simone has small feet and she takes light steps that make shadow imprints while Trip has long and slender feet with determined steps, but not heavy ones. Looking at his own footsteps, he can tell that his prints have a different mark. Taking pictures of all three, he starts to look for the trails.

Before long, he sees where Trip has been resting outside of town. It's a nice open area by a lone tree, which is perfect for looking at the sky as well as the edge of town. Seeing a bare spot that looks like where Trip would lie down, he tries to mimic the pose. Taking a deep breath, Pete is enjoying the view. It's very peaceful and quiet. Although it is hot, it doesn't feel as unbearable as one would think. The breeze makes it feel warm and inviting. After a few minutes, he figures it's time to get back to work. As he looks around, he sees nothing more than prints. There are no traces of hair, wrapper, or any sort of trash in sight.

"At least he cleans up after himself," Pete mutters.

As he gets up to search other areas, he sees a man coming.

"Oh, great!" Pete wonders what he should do now as he stares around in both directions looking for a place to hide.

While he is not sure who is approaching, he suspects that it's Trip. Even though the stranger is not wearing all black, like the man purported to be El Diablo is known to do, his confident walk and style is unmistakable. Although neither of them has ever met the other, they both know that their reputations have preceded them. At the same time, neither one of them knows what the other actually looks like.

Because of her propensity for secrecy, Simone has never introduced them and has made a point of not having their photographs in case someone steals them. She could never forgive herself if she unwittingly let harm fall on either one of them.

Despite being the famous El Diablo, Trip has kept out of the prying eyes of the media, preferring to let an unofficial spokesperson make any public announcements that may be necessary. Instead of remaining in the shadows like many other leaders who do not like the spotlight, he prefers to be far away from any cameras. After all, any detective can tell you that the best way to catch anyone is to look at the crowd. The culprit, or in this case, the modest leader, is always hiding amongst the inconspicuous horde. Even if there is no risk of exposure, he still chooses anonymity any day. He figures his subordinates will make sure that the right message is being sent out to the public and there is no need for him to be present.

Although it is highly unlikely that Trip knows what he looks like, Pete knows that he will figure it out pretty quickly. He will just have to play cool and avoid provoking him. He already knows that he is no match for the famous El Diablo. Putting a little sand on his shirt and face, Pete lies back down on the tree waiting for the man to arrive. Although he has faced many strangers before during his travels, he has never been so nervous to meet someone. He tries to calm himself down by taking deep breaths, but it doesn't seem to be working.

It's not every day that he meets a legend. Closing his eyes, he is trying to still his heart by picturing a serene waterfall and exotic birds. After about a minute, he is glad that it seems to be working, and not a second too soon.

Upon seeing a stranger on his spot, Trip is on high alert, but decides to proceed to the spot. Just like Pete, he is not about to do anything to attract any undue attention.

"Hello," Trip says first upon arriving at the tree.

Squinting his eyes, Pete pretends that he has just woken up and says, "Hm?"

Sitting down, Trip says, "Please don't mind me. I don't mean to disturb you."

Sitting up, Pete clears his throat and says, "Oh, no. It's no problem. I should be on my way anyways. Time a-wasting!"

With that, he dusts his pants off and starts to walk away from Algoma. Seeing that he has no backpacks, no canteen, and no tools of any kind, Trip knows that he is no traveler. Even though he knows that this man is definitely more than meets the eye, he has no intention of engaging him without being provoked first. He simply lies back down and pretends to sleep. He figures the best way to get the man to reveal his identity is to do nothing at all. As always, he is right.

As Pete starts to walk away, he realizes that he is in a bind. He cannot keep walking because he is not prepared for the track on the hot sand. It's not like he has a place to hide and wait until Trip leaves. From the way Trip looks, it's pretty obvious that he is also not going anywhere anytime soon. What should he do? Decisions, decisions.

Hitting his forehead, Pete says, "What a basket case! I am going the wrong way!"

Then, he turns towards Algoma, but then he stops right before he walks toward the secret panel. He realizes that he cannot just go up there using his secret code like he always does. Since only the Elders are supposed to have that kind of access, it would be a dead giveaway that he is not just some random traveler or common tribesman if he uses it. The only other option is to go to the other side of Algoma, where there is a similar panel that he can also use. Although it is a manageable distance, it's going to be quite taxing, especially in the hot sun.

As Pete mutters to himself before beginning the long trek around the city, Trip has confirmed his suspicion that this is no ordinary man and decides to get to the point before he leaves. He gets up and walks toward Pete.

103

"I am Devin, by the way. And you are?" Trip asks.

Since Pete has not expected Trip to introduce himself, he has no idea how to respond. Pete has never been the kind of man who can fly by the seat of his pants. As an architect, he always has to plan everything in detail firs. Hence, he can never handle surprises.

As such, he simply blurts out, "Oh, I am Pete."

As soon as the words come out of his mouth, Pete realizes that it is a mistake to give his real name. After all, he is pretty sure that the man he is speaking with is lying about his real identity.

"Ah, are you the same Pete who has been working with Val?" Trip asks.

Well, since the cat is out of the bag, there is no point denying it. Instead, he needs to look as sincere as possible to get a good impression.

"Yes, yes, I am. I guess my reputation has preceded me. I hope that's a good thing. It's a pleasure to meet you," Pete says with the best fake warm smile that any man can muster.

"Likewise," Trip says with an equally fake smile.

Now that the uncomfortable pleasantry is over, Pete wants to take the opportunity to turn the conversation back on this Devin.

"So, how do you know Val?" Pete asks slyly.

"Who doesn't know the most beautiful woman in town?" Trip answers rhetorically.

"True, true," Pete answers, somewhat dismayed that he has asked a bad question that doesn't yield any additional information from him. Then, he says, "I believe I am at a disadvantage here. It seems you know who I am, but, pardon my ignorance, I don't know anything about you."

"That's not surprising," Trip says with a smile. "There really isn't much to tell. I am really just a nobody."

While to most people, this answer may sound like a brush off, but that is not the case here. Being a private person, he does indeed think of himself as a common man. As far as he is concerned, he is no more special than anyone else on the planet. He sometimes wonders why everyone else is so scared of him. While he is well aware of his reputation and how he got it, he knows that he is just a simple man.

"Oh, come on, don't be so modest. I am sure there is a lot more to you than a nobody," Pete says.

Of course, once again, as soon as he hears himself say it, he already knows that he shouldn't have used those words. If he is indeed talking to the famous El Diablo, he knows that this illusive man hates being patronized. Flattery is the surest way to turn him away. On the other hand, if he does get offended, he would know that it is the famous leader. Looking at his face, Pete smiles awaiting a response.

After a second, Trip returns the smile and says, "Oh, no. I am not being modest. I am just an ordinary guy returning home."

Although Pete is unsuccessful in getting Trip to reveal his true emotions, he is able to get something out of him.

"Ah, home. Is there anything better?" Pete says.

"Nope. There is no place like home," Trip replies automatically as he repeats an old cliché.

"So, where have you traveled to?"

"Oh, here and there."

Not deterred by the non-answer, Pete tries to lead the conversation by saying, "I hear you. I have been to many places, too. I just came back from a place called Balavan. Have you ever been there?"

"Yes, I think so," Trip answers casually.

Delighted that he has taken the bait, Pete tries to reel it in by building some comradeship with him.

"Really? Have you been to the coffee shop on Main Street? It has the best donut I have ever tasted."

"Oh, I will keep that in mind."

"What's your favorite eatery in town?"

"I don't eat out much."

"Really? What's the fun in that? Isn't that part of traveling? To sample different local cuisines?"

"I guess," Trip says with a shrug.

"Where did you stay when you were in town?"

"That hotel on Main Street," Trip answers.

Even though he doesn't know the name of a hotel off hand, it's a safe answer since there is just about everything on that street. Pete knows it, too. All this says is that they both know Balavan well, but Trip still does not like him enough to say anything of use.

Nevertheless, Pete presses and asks, "Do you have a particular place that you like to see when you were in town?"

By now, Trip is well aware that Pete is trying to get him to reveal his true identity. No stranger is that nosey unless he is after something. He is starting to get quite irritated by the incessant line of questioning and figures it's time to go on the offensive.

"Not really. By the way, now that you are done with Val's assignment, what are you doing nowadays?" Trip asks.

"Oh, not much. Just chilling for now," Pete says as he twitches a little.

Although Trip is not an expert at reading faces, he laughs to himself because Pete is showing signs of distress at the question. Despite his insistence, Pete is obviously not as good at this game as he thinks he is.

"Let's cut to the chase, shall we?" Trip asks with a serious voice.

Alarmed, Pete knows he's in well over his head. He cannot even battle Trip in wits right now, for poker for that matter.

"What do you mean?" Pete asks, trying to play dumb.

"You are obviously fishing for information. Why don't you just come out and ask whatever it is you want to ask instead of playing 20 questions with me," Trip says with his arms crossed.

"I… I am sure I don't know what you are talking about."

"Oh, yes, you do."

Flustered, Pete says, "Are you Trip, also known as El Diablo?"

"What if I am?"

From that answer, Pete knows that he is.

"Why are you really here?"

"I don't understand why everyone here thinks I must have some sort of ulterior motive to be here. Like I said, I just want to be home again. Has everyone in Algoma really gone that far off the deep end to find that to be so unbelievable? Why is everyone so suspicious?" Trip rants.

In that instant, Pete seems to understand him and no longer sees him as the scary and ruthless man that he has imagined. Instead, he now sees a man who genuinely misses his childhood home, but is unable to find it. Even though he is physically at the right location, it is surely not the same no matter how similar he manages to make the buildings and the layouts look like the original.

"No, it's not that unbelievable," Pete says.

It's only a few short words, but somehow, they make Trip feel a sense of kinship towards Pete. For some reason, he believes he can trust this man, at least enough not to have to put up his guard every second. Now, he wants to know him better, especially knowing that Simone has trusted him before. Why shouldn't he give him a chance? Who knows? He may be able to help him break down the wall that Drew and his clones are putting up.

"Who are *you* really?" Trip asks casually.

Even though he is not expecting an honest answer, he just has to ask. It's a test, really. If Pete tells the truth, Trip's gut is correct. If not, there is no harm done. He will know that he cannot depend on him for any future endeavors.

"My name really is Pete. I know Simone thinks it's a made up name, like the name Val, but it's not."

Trip sees the mentioning of her real name as a good sign. It seems he has passed the test. For the first time in the conversation, they are starting to be honest with one another.

"Are you really a private investigator?"

"No," Pete answers truthfully. Then, he laughs and says, "That's why Simone is so adorable – such an intelligent, but gullible woman. She hasn't changed a bit."

"So, you knew her when she was little, then," Trip asks.

For a split second, Pete's heart starts to race again. He has inadvertently said something stupid – again.

Nodding, he admits, "Yes, I do."

"Once again, who are you really? Now that you told me what you are *not*, isn't it time you tell me who you *are*?"

108

"Well, we all have our secrets, don't we?"

"Let me see. You don't have an Algomian accent. So, you are not originally from here."

"Neither do you," Pete rebuts.

"True, but I am a native of Algoma. You, on the other hand, probably came here when you are older, possibly an adult, making it difficult to lose your native tongue. If I have to guess, I would say you are from Balavan."

Startled, he says, "How... how can you deduct something like that? My accent is not *that* different from everyone else's."

"It's not just that. It's also the way you went on and on about Balavan, as if you are intimately close to the place. Besides, you are way too old to be one of the natives. Judging from your greyish roots and the crow's feet, you must be what? 48? 49?"

"What? I am *not* that old," Pete says grudgingly.

Although Pete does show some signs of aging, he has always prided himself in being careful about his looks, especially when he is in town. He always makes sure that he dyes his hair before it starts to look grey. Having wavy brown hair that varies from blondish to dark brown, it's difficult to see any grey unless one looks carefully. He also makes precautions against sun damage to minimize wrinkles. Hence, no one has ever doubted that he is in his 30's until now.

Smiling, Trip says, "Then, how old are you?"

"I am 44. Thank you very much."

"Ah, see. That makes you quite a little bit older than any member of the Elders. Doesn't it?"

"So?" Pete says even though he knows exactly where Trip is going with this question.

"As far as I know, there are no survivors of the Great War of 2068 who were older than Drew. That would make you either a spy or a liar. Which are you?"

Although he knows he has been busted, Pete is insulted at the two options that was given and bluntly says, "Neither."

"Then, how do you explain your acceptance into Algoma, considering what a tight ship Drew runs?"

Despite his desire to lie, he decides against it. There is no point. Besides, that would only make Trip right about him being a liar.

"Drew and I are close friends because I helped rebuild this town."

"Ah, so, why is it that our little Simone doesn't know that?"

"I am sure you already know that she doesn't notice many things that are not distinctly obvious."

"Perhaps, but how is that relevant in this case? If you are the builder working with Drew, why is it not obvious to her? She is both a member of the Elders and Drew's wife. That makes her have a need to know, doesn't it?"

"No, actually, it doesn't. She is not a part of the actual building process and my orders are to only let those directly involved know."

"And whose orders are they?"

"I cannot tell you that."

"Why not?"

"The same reason that Drew cannot tell you who the great benefactor is."

"Ah, it's the same person, isn't it?"

"Suffice it to say, yes, it is."

"Why is this benefactor so adamant about anonymity?"

"I really cannot tell you."

"I believe you," Trip says to Pete's surprise.

Ironically, by not saying anything, Trip knows that he is telling the truth. It also tells him something about his character – that he will not betray someone else's trust, which is a definite plus in his book.

"What, that's it? No more questions?" Pete asks skeptically.

"Oh, I didn't say that. Just that I won't press you about the identity of your secret benefactor – for now, anyways."

"Oh."

"Don't look so sad. You are a grown man, for crying out loud," Trip says with a chuckle.

"Well, since we are being honest to one another. Can you please answer me once and for all? Are you El Diablo?"

After a short pause, Trip answers, "Yes."

Taking a deep breath, Pete says, "OK. I am glad we got that out of the way."

"Why is it so important for you to hear me say it? It seems to me that you already knew the answer from the moment you saw me."

Nodding, Pete says, "I want to know which side you are on."

"Does that answer your question?"

"Yes."

"Good. So, which side am I on?"

"The Desiderio's."

"I am hurt by that answer. Are you implying that I am not on your side?"

Nodding, Pete admits.

"Why not?"

"You cannot be for both the Desiderios and the Algomians."

"I don't see why not."

"It's simple. If the Desiderios can defeat Victor's Legionnaires, what is it to stop them from attacking Algoma?"

"That's ridiculous," Trip replies calmly. "Where did you come up with that argument?"

Looking confused, it seems Pete has never thought about it. That is how Amelia thinks and the same definitely goes with Drew. He has always taken that as a fact and never heard anyone argue against it.

"I don't know. That has always been the conventional belief around town," Pete admits.

"Well, I am here to tell you that that is not true."

"How can we be sure of that?"

"You cannot. The only thing is my word. You can either take it or leave it. It doesn't really matter to me. But, I am here to warn you. If you try to attack the Desiderios, you will come to regret it."

The words send a chill down Pete's spine as he takes a big gulp. He cannot believe that the conversation has taken a turn for the worse so quickly. Just a second ago, he thought they could become friends. He has always idolized the man from the minute he heard about him. Who wouldn't? He is brave, strong, intelligent, and seemingly invincible. For a brief moment, he also had the feeling that Trip wanted to befriend him, too, although he is not sure why.

Now, El Diablo is giving him a blatant threat, albeit a well-deserved one. He also knows that El Diablo does not make empty ones. Now that he knows what Pete looks like and his connection to Drew, Trip will not hesitate to make good his promise of retaliation, starting with him, if anything happens to his men.

Now, Amelia is stockpiling weapons. Although she has never explained the reason for this latest project, he is afraid that she is going to use it against Trip's men. After all, it is no secret that El Diablo is responsible for the demise of Amelia's beloved husband.

No matter how he slices it, he knows he is at an impasse. On one hand, he doesn't want to feel the wrath of the great El Diablo, knowing full well that his life depends on it. On the other, he does not want to disappoint Amelia. While it seems like it's a no brainer to the lay man, the choice is not that clear, at least not to him.

Chapter 9: The Mastermind

Pete has long considered Amelia to be his only friend and family. Hence, all of this time, he has been blindly following her commands and never really questions anything she says. Over the years, he has had no reason to doubt her. Everything she has commanded has been for the good of Algoma.

"But, has it really?" Pete asks himself for the first time since he met the illustrious Mrs. Richardson.

There have definitely been positive improvements since she has arrived. Obviously, without her, there would not even be a town left, let alone a thriving one. There is also little doubt that, under her tutelage, the children of Algoma have, in most part, grown up to be upstanding citizens. Yet, even Pete cannot ignore the fact that there is a sense of ominous paranoia in town.

At that moment, his ashen expression says it all. Trip has given him fair warning and plenty to think about. There is no point staying any longer. Considering that they both know each other's true identities, there is also no point in hiding the fact that they both have a way to get into Algoma without having to listen to Drew's veiled intimidation act. With nothing else left to say, Trip gets up to go back to his rental home and resumes his life as Devin, the average run of the mill builder.

"Wait. Please don't leave yet," Pete begs with a solemn voice.

Turning around, Trip simply looks at him without saying a word. Nervous, Pete knows that he needs to choose his next words carefully, but really has no idea where to start. If he leaves it like that, he may have turned Trip into an unwilling enemy, which spells bad news for him and everyone else in Algoma. Even though it is his childhood home, it's pretty clear that it's not the physical location that matters to Trip, but the people in it. From what he has seen and knows about El Diablo so far, the only one he cares about here is Simone.

Back in Balavan, however, he has every member of the Desiderios, especially his beloved Warrior. The choice seems simple. If he has to defend one, it will certainly not be Algoma.

Ironically, by being too careful, he has missed his chance to say his piece. Sensing his hesitation, Trip turns away again.

Realizing that he must say something now, Pete gets up to follow him and blurts out, "Look, I personally have no intention of hurting anyone."

Trip slows his pace, but continues walking. Although he suspects they are true, these words mean very little to him. Judging from his intelligent, but awkward conversation, he already knows that Pete is not the master mind behind it all, certainly not behind any form of violence. The question is who? If anything, he is the brain who stands in the back – way back.

Even a fool like Drew is more likely to plot against Balavan than he is, but somehow he doubts it is him. While Drew appears to be a first class jerk on the surface, he knows that he cares deeply about his family and would never put their lives at risk unnecessary. There has to be someone else.

"I am sorry if I have offended you." Pete says as he interrupts Trip's thought.

Even though begging for forgiveness usually works, it certainly does not seem to be the case here. Instead of finding it sincere, Trip is a little irritated that Pete thinks he can be offended by mere words. It's much bigger than that.

He has just learned that his childhood home is trying to attack his adopted one. Right now, he needs to focus his attention on finding out how as quickly as possible instead of listening to this loser try to apologize for triviality.

To do that, he needs to get Pete to spill the beans without looking like he is doing it. The first thing to do is to continue the charade and storm off as if he has been insulted deeply. That way, Pete will have to go the extra mile to win him over. With Trip walking away faster, Pete is not sure what to do. All he can think of is to try to keep pace with him. Being a middle-aged architect, however, he is not in nearly as good of shape as Trip is. Before long, he is panting. Nevertheless, he does not give up as he begins to jog in order to keep up with him.

When Trip finally stops at the access panel, Pete tries to engage him again and says, "Please. Tell me what I need to do to mend the fence."

Sensing that Pete is at his most vulnerable, Trip stops and says, "For starters, you need to tell me what is going on."

Not realizing that he is being played, Pete is delighted that Trip is actually talking to him again.

"If I do, can you promise to keep it to yourself?"

"Why should I?" Trip says coldly.

Looking at the ground, Pete shows a definite sign of frustration and utters the only thing he can think of, "For the sake of the children."

Although he does not mean to do it, Pete has struck a nerve. At that moment, Trip thinks back to the days when he was an orphan and how a war had destroyed him. Then, his thought immediately turns to Simone's little ones and how happy they both look in their cozy little home with their father. He cannot let them face the same devastation

116

that he and their parents endured. Nevertheless, Trip is not about to let Pete think that he has won him over with that simple statement.

"What about the children of Balavan?" Trip asks.

At that moment, Pete also thinks back to his childhood. Unbeknownst to Trip, they were both orphans. While they both had terrible experiences growing up, however, the circumstances were very different. Unlike Trip who lost his parents in bloodshed, Pete never knew his. Abandoned at birth, he was left on the doorsteps of a church swaddled in a light blue blanket with nothing when he was merely a day old. There was no note and no way of finding his birth parents. Like many abandoned children, he went to the window every day, hoping that his parents would show up to reclaim him. But, that day never came.

Instead, he imagined that his parents were superheroes who could not come because they were in faraway places saving lives and could not reveal themselves to him. But, they would sneak in in the middle of the night to gaze upon their child. At least that was what he was hoping for. Every time he would hear a noise in the orphanage, his hope would be up, hoping to see them, but they also never happened. After years of disappointment, he began to think that his parents had fallen in the line of duty. Perhaps, their last words were regrets that they never got to know their son.

Unfortunately, by holding on to this belief, it also prevented him from being adopted. Because he had always hoped that his real parents would come for him, he always acted out when potential new parents come to visit. His defiant attitudes towards them made sure that he stayed in the orphanage. As he grew older, however, he started to realize that perhaps his parents were just deadbeats who didn't care enough about him to look for him.

The thought turned him bitter. By then, those who are looking to adopt began to look for children younger than him. To make matters worse, he faced ridicule from other children constantly. While some of the other orphans coped by acting out or using humor, he stayed in his shell.

Like Trip, he became a loner, shielding himself from others. But, unlike Trip, he found comfort in tinkering with gadgets and finding out how they work rather than by learning how to defend himself from being hurt again. He would take things apart and try to put them back together. Of course, this resulted in him being punished quite often when he was younger for breaking every appliance he could get his hands on. By the time he was old enough to leave the orphanage, he was at the level of a professional engineer.

Although they have more things in common than either one of them realizes, Pete does not feel the same for the people of Balavan as he does those in Algoma. To him, the difference is like night and day. The Balavians are a bunch of privileged snobs who made fun of him when he needed a friend the most while the Algomian are victims who needed to be saved. Yet, here is Trip, who is both. Should he follow El Diablo's lead and forgive those who have trespassed against him?

But, wait, Trip didn't forgive Victor. No, sir. It's quite the opposite. He crushed him and obliterated those who followed him. How is what Amelia is planning on doing any different?

Seeing that Pete is again in deep thought to the other tangent, Trip knows that he needs to get him back in. Snapping his fingers, Trip says, "Hello, are you still there?"

After seeing Trip's cold stare, he snaps out of it and remembers that he is trying to align with him, not to alienate him.

118

"Oh, I am sorry. I got distracted," Pete says. "How about let's just say that it's for the sake of peace for both sides. Would you be willing to entertain that?"

"Well, duh. Obviously," Trip thinks to himself. That has been his position from the beginning. Pete is the one talking about launching a disruption of that peace, not him.

"Fine," Trip finally says, "I will tentatively agree to keep it to myself, but if I hear anything detrimental to Balavan, I make no promises."

Nodding, Pete is somewhat relieved as he says, "Agreed."

Truth be told, Pete does want to tell Trip everything. The more he thinks about it, the more he begins to second guess her motives. With no real enemies, there is really no reason for a stockpile of weapons and military crafts. In fact, it can backfire on them. What if a renegade or spy gets a hold of the weaponries and use them against them? That would be unthinkable. It took decades to physically rebuild Algoma the first time. Even then, the emotional wounds are still deep in many of its people. That is why Drew and many others still hold such a grudge against outsiders.

Putting his trust in Trip to be fair, Pete takes a deep breath and says, "Come on. Let's go somewhere where there are no prying eyes and ears."

*

Going through the same motion that Simone did earlier to enter Algoma, Pete puts his hand over the access panel. They both cross bridge without incident. Trip is curious as to why no one bothered to stop them or question why the two of them are together. Aren't Drew's security team watching the bridge area like a hawk? As he ponders the answer, he looks at his new partner and notices that he is shining.

"Like it?" Pete asks with a smile.

"What is it?"

"It's my new camouflage system. To those within a foot of it, it looks like ordinary people wearing their usual clothing, but as you step further away, you begin to disappear."

With that being said, Pete does a little impromptu demonstration by stepping away. Impressed, Trip is both excited and troubled by this new invention. If enemy forces attack Balavan in that disguise, they are as good as dead. On the other hand, if he can team up with him, he may be able to convince his new partner to share the technology. Looking up into the sky and the surrounding areas, Trip is trying to see if he can figure out his secret.

"Interested?" Pete asks as he smiles, knowing full well that he is.

"Perhaps," Trip says calmly, knowing full well that Pete would certainly ask for something in return and he is not prepared to offer anything right now.

A little dismayed by Trip's show of disinterest, Pete gets in the elevator. Expecting to emerge in the same little house that he saw when he was with Simone, Trip is surprised to find that he is looking at an oasis surrounded by desert. He doesn't remember seeing anything like this from outside of town. It must be well hidden.

"Welcome to my sanctuary," Pete says.

"Where are we?"

"In the heart of Algoma."

Rolling his eyes, Trip cannot believe Pete actually answers with such an obvious but useless answer. Then, he realizes what it is that he is looking at and begins to understand what Pete is saying. Can it be? Instead of the bright beautiful buildings that can be seen from the outside, which are mere replicas that had to be rebuilt after the war, can they actually be in the middle of an *original* piece of his childhood home? Possibly the only one? He distinctly remembers an oasis just like this one when he was young. The water was calm, crisp, and fresh. There was an abundant amount of palm trees surrounding it.

"Is this what I think it is?" Trip asks without explaining what he is thinking.

As if there is no need to explain, Pete nods and says, "Yes, it is. Is it as beautiful as it was back then?"

Nodding, Trip reaches his hand into the water to scoop some to drink. The cool liquid brings back memories. It's definitely the same. It is sweeter than any other water he has ever tasted. Like it or not, this *is* home. Then, a thought comes to mind. What is home without family? Where are the graves? What happened to his parents' bodies?

Now that the town is rebuilt, he has not seen a cemetery. Of course, at the time of the war, there was no formal burial place. Everyone would bury their loved ones close to their homes. He vaguely remembers the spot where his parents fell during the war and the place where he buried them, but now that everything has been built on top, did they leave the bodies where they lie?

"Go ahead. Ask me," Pete says as if he knows that Trip has a million questions in mind.

"What did you do with the dead?"

"I personally didn't do anything with them. I wasn't part of the rebuilding process until months later, but from what I heard, they gathered all of the corpses lying on the ground and buried them in a mass grave underground."

"Lying on the ground." That means they didn't do anything to his parents' bodies since he had buried them before wandering off.

"Is the town above an exact replica of the original?" Trip asks.

"Since I am not from here, I have no first-hand knowledge of the layout of the town, but I did my best to get the most accurate descriptions. Of course, they were all from children eleven and under. That means there can be room for a lot of inaccuracies," Pete admits.

Of course, Trip doesn't care about authenticity. All he is thinking about right now is paying his respects to his parents. He has not thought about visiting their final resting place since he left. That is not to say that he hasn't thought about them. He has, quite frequently, in fact, but because he gets angry every time he thinks about them, he has trained himself not to over the years. Although he has a sudden urge to see them and tell them about his life, he knows that this is not the time or place.

"OK, now that we are here. Let's get down to business," Trip says.

Pete has been trying to delay the moment for as long as he can, but it seems there is no point deferring any longer.

Clearing his throat, he says, "What exactly do you want to know?"

"What I really want to know if who is pulling the strings in this operation, but I already know that you will not tell me. So, I am going to ask you this. Why are you protecting this person?"

"Because she is the greatest thing that has happened to Algoma," Pete says proudly.

"Ah, she," Trip says.

Covering his mouth, Pete cannot believe he let that slip already. In that one simple sentence, he has already revealed the gender of the benefactor. There are only so many female leaders of note in Balavan. He is hoping that Trip will not figure it out.

"So, what is it that she does that demands anonymity?"

"She has her own reasons."

"Fine," Trip knows that he has to ask a different kind of question if he wants to figure out her true identity. "Why do you have such loyalty to her?"

"Because she is a dear friend."

"How did you two become so close that you would do so much for her? Is she a girlfriend?"

Blushing, Pete says, "Don't be ridiculous! She is a good 15 years older than I am!"

"Ah, another valuable clue," Trip says to himself. That would make her what, around 60 years old or so.

"Oh, come on! Just because she's a few years older than you doesn't mean you can't be attracted to her," Trip teases as he tries to get him to open up even more.

"Oh, no, I couldn't possibly," Pete says as he frantically waves his hands in denial before adding, "She is a widow."

While that may seem like an innocent remark, it isn't. Although she is of advanced age, she is not so old that her husband would have died of old age yet. Trip is keeping that in mind as well as he builds his profile on this mystery woman.

"I am sorry to hear that," Trip says.

"Oh, don't worry about it. We never even met."

"Ah, so the husband does not know of his existence," Trip says to himself.

Why would a man and a woman who does not have a romantic or physical relationship need to stay away from the husband? There can be several possibilities. One possible answer is that the husband is extremely jealous.

While this can be a reasonable cause, one would think that the woman would break off the relationship if it really bothers her husband that much. In all probability, there is a bigger reason for this ruse.

Perhaps, her husband is an important figure and she wants to keep Pete in the dark about him. Or, perhaps, this woman simply wants to keep her personal and business lives separate.

From the way that Pete is protecting her, however, Trip cannot help but feel that their relationship is not as platonic as he makes it sound.

That can certainly explain the blushing when he vehemently denied *having* a relationship with her. If that is the case, Trip wants to leave that one alone. He is the last person who wants to be tangled in someone else's messy love life.

"How did you two meet?"

"She found me."

Yet, another clue. It sounds like this woman certainly has the know-how to find talent. Most women with money often simply advertise when they need to recruit someone. She is different. She does not take any chances by waiting for them to come to her.

She has to research and find the right one on her own. That also makes her quite possessive and controlling. Is that why he does everything she asks without question? Has she trained him to follow directions blindly? How many others does she have under her spell?

"You must be very special, then, huh?" Trip says half-heartedly.

"Aw, that's very sweet of you to say, but I don't see myself as such," Pete replies humbly, not realizing that Trip meant it as sarcasm than a compliment.

"Any idea how she found you?"

"Not really. I never asked."

"Why not? I thought you two are close," Trip asks as if he is being a curious little boy.

"I don't know. I guess it's one of those things that if you don't ask at a certain time, it just feels awkward to do it later. You know what I mean?"

Nodding, Trip certainly does. What he has learned is that while Pete considers this woman a confidant, there is a certain amount of fear that is mixed in their relationship where he is afraid to do certain things in order to not make sure that he does not upset her. It's kind of dysfunctional, actually, when one person has to walk on eggshells for the other.

Being careful not to be too obvious, Trip continues, "Besides rebuilding Algoma, what else do you do for her?"

"Anything she asks."

"That's a pretty tall order. Like what?" Trip asks casually as if he really doesn't care what the answer is.

Thinking for a second, Pete knows that this is a tricky question to answer. He doesn't want to say anything that will betray Amelia's confidentiality, but at the same time, he wants to be honest with Trip if he intends on building a positive relationship with him.

"Hm, for example, once, I followed a guy to find out what kind of person he is."

"Interesting. Doesn't she have other people who do that kind of work for her? I mean, that doesn't sound like a job that an architect or engineer should be doing."

"Well, she doesn't trust very many people when it comes to matters of Algoma."

"So, what makes her trust you so much?"

"I don't really know. I guess it's just a feeling of mutual respect. After we worked together for so long, we kind of just understand each other. You know, kind of like you and the Warrior. I am sure," Pete says with a sheepish grin.

"Why does everyone have to mention her in every discussion?" Trip laments.

It's precisely because they have a close relationship that it's awkward to hear about it from every stranger who knows his identity. In any case, Trip can tell that this conversation has turned to the mushy side and he has no intention of going down that road. So far, he has gathered enough information on this mystery benefactor to make an educated guess on her identity.

The fact that he disappears for weeks on end, most probably to meet this mystery woman, means that she is most likely also from Balavan. Who else in his adopted town fits that description besides the wife of his nemesis, Victor Richardson? What's more? He now realizes that she is not just the benefactor, but is also the mastermind behind it all.

Despite having figured out the identity of the mysterious woman, Trip keeps it cool. He knows that this is only the first piece of the puzzle. He needs to figure out her plans.

Changing subject, Trip asks, "What about what you are building in the test stage? They look like overkill for self-defense."

"You are right. They are not simply for self-preservation," Pete admits.

"So, are you going to admit that you are planning on attacking my adopted home?"

"No, I am not," Pete says. After a short pause, he adds, "But I cannot guarantee that the benefactor is not."

"It's one thing for you not to tell me who she is. It's another to tell me that you are not willing to help prevent blood shed of thousands of innocent lives," Trip responds chillingly.

Shuddering at the sound of his words, Pete shakes his head and whispers, "I am not a monster."

"That's why you need to help me prevent this war from happening. I know you can."

Turning away, Pete stares at the glistening of the calm water under the sun. He is truly at crossroads. He sincerely wants to help Trip, but he just cannot get himself to do it. He cannot even get himself to *say* that he is willing to help him. It's as if the words being spoken itself are a betrayal in itself.

"Can you let me think about it?" Pete pleads.

Understanding his dilemma, Trip nods and says, "Till we meet again" before taking off.

Before Pete can reply, Trip is gone. He looks around for a trace of the man, but cannot seem to find him. He is surprised that the man is able to disappear so quickly, especially in a land that Pete has built and one that Trip should be unfamiliar with. Last time when Trip turned away, he merely walked. Was it all an act to get Pete to stop him? It must be. Shuddering at the thought again, Pete is more impressed with Trip than ever before. He knows that El Diablo is truly a man to be reckoned with and any sign of weakness in the man is merely a mirage in itself.

Chapter 10: Home vs. Home

As Trip disappears, he follows his instinct to go to the only place he can think of at the moment – his parents' resting place. Although he cannot remember the exact location, he lets his intuition lead him. Just like earlier when he was getting closer to Algoma, he gets the same gut wrenching feeling when he is close. As he walks past a familiar looking building, he stops as a flash of memories flood through his mind, from the curdling sound of screams to the stickiness of old blood and the stench of death, most of all, the sinister laughter of Victor's men while they slaughter his kinsman.

Gritting his teeth, he looks at the ground. Without thinking, he begins to dig with nothing but his hands, just like the way he did so many years ago. Before long, he comes across what he is looking for – human remains. There is nothing left of them but skeletons. Even their clothes and moccasins have since decomposed. Despite a lack of any other forms of identification, he knows they were his parents. He distinctively remembers putting them next to one another when he buried them with his tiny and bloody hands. Even though every part of him wants to mourn for them, he does not allow himself to. Instead, he carefully picks up every piece of them and put them in his sack.

He has to give them a proper burial somewhere respectable. Back then, he didn't have the time or the energy to find the right place. He simply dug a hole in the nearest spot that has a clearing. It was in building buildings where people could walk all over them. Just the thought that hundreds of people probably trampled over them in the past two decades saddens him. It's no fault of theirs, of course. How can strangers know that there are two loving parents buried down there? It's the middle of nowhere.

128

Now, he must do it properly. It's the least he can do as a dutiful son.

As he finishes the painful task and covers the ground back up, he notices Pete coming his way from the corner of his eye. Apparently, Pete is more insightful than he appears when he is not intimidated. Even though he has not seen which direction El Diablo went, he is able to deduce from their conversation which way he may have headed. While it took him some time, he eventually finds him.

Even though knowing the layout of the land certainly helps, it is still quite impressive for someone like him to pinpoint a location in a place this big. Upon his arrival, Pete remains silent as he stands a good distance away from Trip to give him room. He has a good idea what Trip is doing right now and the last thing he wants to do is to interrupt the sacred moment.

"Are you ready to resume our conversation?" Trip asks without looking at him.

Surprised that he has been seen, Pete clears his throat and says, "I am sorry to interrupt. Please finish what you are doing first."

"What makes you think I am doing something?" Trip asks rhetorically as he walks towards him. Then, lightheartedly, he says, "Have you been spying on me?"

Waving frantically, Pete denies it and says, "Of course not! I wasn't *spying*. I was simply looking for you."

"Well, you have found me. Unless you are ready to talk, I will be on my way."

As soon as he sees Pete lower his head, Trip already has his answer. With that he leaves again. This time, he heads back home, the other home, to Balavan, while leaving Pete standing there unsure of what to do next. At least, he has bought some time and does not have to give him an answer just quite yet.

*

Trip walks off, heading back to Balavan. There was no longer any place for his parents in Algoma. He stepped out into the sand and started walking toward Balavan.

He traveled lightly, with only enough supplies to get him through the trip, so it wasn't long before he made it there.

As soon as he arrives, Trip heads straight to his beloved garden. Before he enters it, he smiles because *this* is truly home. The delicate scent and the serenity have no comparison, not any more anyways. Once upon a time before Victor ruined everything, there was.

Now, everything in Algoma is nothing but a replica. Despite the gallant effort that Pete has made to duplicate everything, it's just not the same. The only thing worth saving now is the oasis and what is in his sack behind him right now. Looking very solemn, he looks for a place where he can finally lay his parents to rest.

Then, he sees the perfect spot. It's partially covered by a cherry tree. When the sun hits it, the light flickers. When the blossom falls, it looks as if it's dancing down to the ground. For some reason, there are few flowers in that area, as if it is reserved for a higher purpose. As he sits by the tree, he marvels at the beauty of the garden.

This has to be the place. Even though they have never stepped foot in Balavan when they were alive, Trip thinks they would be pleased to be here in his new home.

"Welcome home, stranger!" a familiar voice says cheerfully as she runs towards him.

With a sad smile, he says, "How do you know I am here?"

"How do I always?" Violet says as she gives him a big hug.

Discounting his facial expression as exhaustion, she steps back and is taken aback by what she sees.

"Wow, that trip of yours certainly did a number on you, didn't it? I love it!" Violet exclaims.

For a second, he is not sure what she is talking about. Then, he realizes she is referring to his clothes. He is still wearing the bright outfit that he wore when he was trying to be in character as Devin. It's exactly the kind of ensemble that Violet has been trying to get him to wear for some time, but she has never imagined that he would ever do so. Within seconds, however, her cheerfulness turns seriousness as she realizes that it's not just exhaustion on his face. She knows that look and it's usually bad news.

"What's wrong?"

For the next hour, he gives her a rundown of the new Algoma, from the insanely impenetrable underground town and access panels to his uncomfortable meeting with Drew and Simone. Of course, he conveniently leaves out the part about his past friendship with Simone. It's not that he is afraid Violet may not like the news or be uncomfortable knowing that he had someone besides her in his life.

It's that he figures it's best to provide only the facts for now. At least, that's what he tells himself. She listens intently like a child until he gets to the part about Pete and the stockpile of military grade items and Amelia's involvement.

Concerned, she ponders, "How can this be? I always thought she is just an old socialite who needs her husband's connections to do anything. I guess she has us all fooled."

Then, she looks up and says, "Think Thom is up to the task?"

"Doubtful."

"I know."

Violet knows that she is definitely pushing it by asking whether or not Thom is going to spy on his mother. He has already betrayed his adopted father and birth father. It would kill him to betray another parent. He is tormented enough as it is. There is no telling if one more betrayal will drive him over the edge. With his skills and knowledge about everything that goes on in Balavan, he can be quite a formidable and destructive foe if pushed to it. It's better to be safe and keep him out of this one, at least for now.

"We need to use someone else who can get close to Amelia," Violet concludes. "What about your new friend Simone?"

"What about her?" Trip asks curiously.

After having told Violet about her gullibility, he is surprised that she would even suggest her as a spy for this mission.

"I figure since she is a co-leader of the new Algoma, she should have the networks and the resources to stop the attack."

"It's easier said than done."

"If I didn't know better, I say you are trying to protect her," Violet says slyly. After staring into his eyes for another second, she exclaims, "I am right, aren't I? You *are* protecting her! Come on! Spill the beans! Did something happen between the two of you that you are not telling me?"

"Don't be ridiculous. She's a married woman with two children," Trip says seriously.

"I don't mean just now. You can tell me. Was she your little childhood crush? Were you two sitting under a tree? K-I-S-S-I-N-G? Fess up! I won't tell anyone," Violet says jokingly.

"No, nothing of that sort. I simply knew her when we were children. There, are you happy now?"

Even though it started out as a tease, hearing him confess that he did know this woman does sting, just a little bit. Even though he only admits to knowing her existence, she knows it's more than that. He never remembers *anybody* unless this person is important to him, especially after two long decades. This woman must be quite special. The thought kind of bothers Violet, even though she is ashamed to admit it. She has never seen him as a *man* before who may be interested in the fairer sex. Instead, she has always considered him, for a lack of better word, a part of her. It's a bit uneasy, and quite new to her. Yet, she knows that eventually he will want to start a family of his own. When that day comes, she may not be in the picture, even though she hopes that she will.

Gathering her thoughts, she chastises herself, "So what if he knows her. It's really none of your business, especially when it's ancient history. Get a hold of yourself!"

Trying to get back on track with the conversation, she says, "What I am saying is that since already know her, we should be able to count on her to help us now that we have established the fact that you don't think she can handle it by herself."

Relieved that she has dropped the subject that encroaches his personal life, Trip simply nods.

"So, when are you going to make the introduction?"

"Later, or maybe never. I am not sure if she is the right one yet."

"Well, if not her, who?"

"We may be able to use this Pete."

"What? But he sounds like Amelia's right hand man. What makes you think we can trust him?"

"It's just a feeling. Nothing more."

Violet knows that Trip is very good with feelings. He has proven it over and over again in the battlefields before, saving many lives, including hers. If he senses that there is an enemy coming from a certain direction, everyone in the Desiderios knows to move – fast, if they know what is good for them. By now, Trip's sixth sense is as good as fact to them. Even so, she wants to know what his plans are with this Pete. As far as she is concerned, he is nothing more than a spy acting as an ally.

"When can I meet him?" Violet says sternly.

She is not about to let this charlatan infiltrate her men.

"I am sure he will make himself available soon enough."

Violet knows what that means, which troubles her even more. People who show up on their own usually do so with a plan in mind. Nevertheless, she trusts Trip. If he says he can trust him, she will try to, too, at least for now.

After a moment of silence, Trip simply says, "Can we talk about it later? I have another business to attend to."

With that, Trip disappears, as usual. Violet wonders what is more important than a potential attack on Balavan, but leaves it alone. She knows he has his reasons. He always does. Before long, Trip returns to his room to change back to his normal black clothes. When he was in the new Algoma, he had no problem with wearing bright outfits as a disguise. He doesn't really know why, but he has a sneaky suspicion that it's because it reminds him of Violet. By dressing like that, he feels like she is next to him and he can conquer anything on his own. Now that he actually is next to her, he no longer needs it.

As soon as he changes, he senses that Violet is already in his room and says, "Did you forget something?"

Smiling, she says, "As much as I like your new duds, I have to say, black does suit you better."

"Thanks," he says flatly as he continues to groom himself.

"So, what's the occasion?"

Even though Violet is trying not to let the thought of Simone get the best of her, she is still curious as to why her best friend has suddenly decided to clean up. As long as she has known him, he has never cared how he looks and hardly spends anytime with a shaver or comb, for that matter. His daily hygiene routine typically consists of a two minute shower followed by another two minute session of teeth brushing.

"Look in the sack."

Now that certainly piques Violet's interest. Like a little girl, she gets a sudden gush of excitement as if it's Christmas morning. What in the world can he have brought back with him from Algoma. Did he actually buy her something? That would be terribly sweet of him, but not like him, not at all. He never cares to show his gratitude, friendship, or anything with material goods.

Nevertheless, what can he possible want her to see that would require him to be cleaned up? Can it be? No... It cannot. It cannot possibly be a ring. He cannot possibly be asking her to *marry* him.

While the thought is definitely very inviting, she knows that is no change that it can be true – none, nil, absolute not. He has never uttered a word of romance to her before.

He cannot possibly spring a question like that out of nowhere.

So, what else can it be? As she looks at the sack, her excitement instantly goes away. There is mud all over it and it's bumpy and bulging. Because of the tightness of the sack, she can see that there is something straight, about three feet long with a round nob at the end. What can that be? Standing back for a second. She knows exactly what that is before she ever touches the sack. It's not a wedding that he is looking forward to, it's a funeral. That must be a leg bone. It makes sense. That's why he is back to his usual black and solemnness so quickly. It's not just the imminent news of attack that he received in the new Algoma.

"I am sorry," Violet says gloomily. "I am here for you. Whatever you need."

"I know."

Going to her room, Violet changes to a black shirt and making a few phone calls before returning. At sunset, the two of them hold a private funeral for his parents in his beloved garden. Few words are said – openly anyways. Everything Trip has to say he pretty much keeps to himself. Even now, he still will not shed any tears. He is done with that. He is just glad that his parents are finally close to him and he can visit them as often as he wishes. He is also glad that his best friend is there for him for such a momentous occasion without needing to ask.

After the ceremony, the two of them to their respective rooms to change back to their usual attire, down to Trip's tussled hair. Even though neither one of them is in the mood to eat, they know that everyone will be there. It's as good of a time as any to let everyone know that their illustrious leader has returned, for now, anyways. As expected, everyone welcomes Trip home with open arms. Some pretend to punch him in the gut while others pat him in the back or simply give him a hearty handshake.

136

Regardless of the actual greeting received, one thing is for sure.

"This is what it should feel like when you are *home*," Trip says to himself with a faint smile on his lips.

*

While Trip has returned to those who love and respect him, Pete is pondering what he should do next. He is sure that he has infuriated the mighty El Diablo. He cannot go and tell Amelia about it. There is no telling what she would do. Considering that she can be quite temperamental at times, she may act rashly and cause further harm than good. He cannot go to Simone because she doesn't really understand what's going on. By going to her, she is more likely to expose him than anything else. What else can he do?

The thought returns to Trip. Even though he is trying to forge an alliance with him, Pete still has an urge to find out more about the man. Considering what a private man he is, the best way to learn more about him is to ask someone who knows him, but that is a dangerous move. What if he finds out? The alliance is sure to be broken before it's ever started. The second best option is to search his home. Even though he knows that it is morally wrong, he just cannot help it. He knows that this is as good of a time as any to check him out. Based on what he has seen in their last meeting, he figures El Diablo should be busy reburying his parents right now. Nothing else would be on his mind when he is preoccupied with such a heavy task.

Remembering that Trip has told him that he is renting a home under the name Devin, Pete goes to his secret surveillance shack in the testing area. Searching through records, it doesn't take him long to find out which home it is. As he reaches the rental property, he is a little nervous. Even though he is pretty sure no one is there, he is still afraid to go in, just in case he is wrong. With the mood he would be in, Pete has no intention of facing Trip's wrath. After standing outside for a minute, however, he figures it's safe to go in. If El Diablo is indeed home, he would have confronted him by now. After a customary knock that is unanswered, he looks around to make sure that no one is watching him because using his special code to open the door. Being the architect of a town definitely has its benefits – and secrets.

As he walks inside, he sees the abode of a very lonely man. There is nothing besides the furnishing that comes with the simple house. Every piece of furniture belongs to the landlord. Opening the refrigerator, it is also completely empty. How can a man live without a single morsel of food anywhere? Even if he does not know how to cook, there is usually something in the fridge, like take-outs, beer, or at least a bottle of clean water to drink. Judging from his lean physique, Pete wonders if the man actually does not eat anything at all.

"Since he *is* El Diablo, perhaps he eats human souls instead," Pete mumbles to himself.

Either that, or this house is nothing but a prop that he uses as a front when necessary, which is the more probable reason. Inside the bathroom, there is a plain white towel, a bar of soap, and a black toothbrush. All of which look clean, dry, and unused. The roll of toilet paper is still tacked together at the end while the sink and the tub are in pristine condition, as if it has just been thoroughly scrubbed. There is not a single hair or even water spot to be seen. In the bedroom, the bed is neatly made and the pillow is perfectly fluffed, as if it has never been slept in since he rented the place. Either that or he is the neatest man on earth, bar none. Judging from the fact that he has no problem with

138

mud during their earlier encounter, this is highly unlikely. Besides, there is also no trace of any clothes either.

Pete wonders if Trip has ever actually lived there at all. *Live* may be too strong of a word. Considering that he has left a toothbrush, it is probably a sign that he has at least *slept* in the domicile once or at least gives the illusion that he has. Considering that Trip has left no real clues behind, Pete decides to sit on the couch, to give himself a moment to think. Alas, nothing is coming to him. All he knows is that he is starting to feel thirsty. Boredom can do that to a man. Since he is already here, he might as well get some water.

"Oh, right, the only thing is faucet water," he laments as he rolls his eyes.

No matter, he is not that picky. Since he knows the source of the water and how it's being purified, he is more than willing to take it straight right out of the tap, but he is not about to lap it like the family pet. Instinctively, he looks into the cabinet for a glass, but finds none.

Slapping his head, he mumbles, "Duh, why do I bother?"

Unless the landlord has left some dishes, he is pretty sure there is none around. Nevertheless, he figures there is nothing else for him to do. Since he is already prying, he might as well be thorough. After opening on drawer after another, it's all the same. Everything is empty. He even looks under the cushions and under the bed. There is not even a dead bug or lint anywhere. Then, he opens the cabinet under the sink, just for grins. To his surprise, there is a small trashcan in there.

"Hm, landlord must have left that there," he whispers.

Putting his detective cap on, he thinks, "Don't all of the great detectives look through people's trash for clues? Of course, he wouldn't leave any."

Half-heartedly, he tips the can to see if there is anything inside. For the second time today, he is surprised that it makes a clank noise. There *is* something in there. Taking it out for a closer look, he sees an empty black bottle that looks like an average beer bottle with no labels on it.

"So, the man does drink beer, after all," Pete mutters.

As he is about to return the wastebasket back in its place, he stops. Something doesn't feel right. Why would Trip drink beer? He doesn't look like the kind who would touch alcohol. He is definitely too uptight to put such filth in his body. To have a completely empty refrigerator, why would he have one solidary empty bottle of beer in the trash? Despite his better judgment, he hesitantly takes the bottle out with just his thumb and index finger, trying to touch as little of it as possible. He looks inside, there is a few drops left. Then, he sniffs it.

"Mmmm," Pete says out loud without realizing it.

It actually smells pretty good, but he cannot tell what it is. It kind of smells like some sort of broth but with tons of different flavors in it. He cannot tell if it's sweet, sour, spicy, or something else. It's as if it's all of the above. Curious as to what this concoction is, he carefully puts the lid back on and puts it in his shirt jacket. Even if it's nothing but his dinner, it's the only clue he has, and a puzzling one at that. Why would El Diablo drink this thing? What is it? Is it an energy drink? Is it a secret formula for eternal youth? Is it simply a liquefied dinner, like the kind astronauts have? Or, is it poison left in the trashcan to trick nosy people like him. After all, since he cleans up after himself so well, why would he leave a bottle? He could have easily taken it with him like he does everything else. The thought is a little chilling, but still exciting. Regardless of what it is, one thing is for sure. He has never seen something like this before.

Before leaving, he ponders whether or not he should put one of his well hidden surveillance systems in the home,
140

but decides against it. It's pretty useless considering that Trip has no intention of using it. Besides, because the home is in such a busy part of the town, it is highly unlikely that he would invite anyone else into the house. Even if he does, it would most certainly be for show. If that is the case, the footage from that kind of surveillance will only serve as a distraction from what his real intention is. Satisfied with his decision, he walks away happy that he has not left empty handed.

Chapter 11: Hidden Friendship

Even though there is no shortage of chemists and scientists in Algoma, Pete has no intention of letting anyone in town know that he has Trip's mystery bottle. Actually, he doesn't want anyone to know that he is in contact with the famous El Diablo at all. The less others know about them, the better, at least until he figures out his plan. For now, he has to get its contents analyzed as soon as possible and as far away from Algoma as he can. Even if it's just to satisfy his curiosity, he has to do it. Just like Trip, he has a hunch about this bottle.

If not Algoma, where? The only other place that he knows well is Balavan, Trip's town. Is it worth the risk? Then again, how much risk are we talking about? If it is just broth, there is no harm done. Nobody cares about a secret recipe for delicious soup, at least not for a military man like Trip. It's not like he has a desire to open a restaurant or win a culinary award of some sort. But, if he does, Pete certainly wants to be there to witness it. The thought is so ridiculous that he starts to laugh out loud in the streets of the new Algoma. He hasn't realized his outburst until he sees some people staring at him.

If it's a special tonic made for enhancing energy or improving health, it's the same. Those things are everywhere. Just go to any grocery store and you can find dozens of different variations of them, each claiming to be better than the rest. Unless Trip plans on opening an energy store, no one would really care if Pete finds out the recipe. Besides, it's not like he is going to mass produce it and market it as his own. Once he figures out that it's just a common drink, he will be satisfied knowing what it is, and destroy any evidence that he ever knew about it before Trip finds out.

If it's poison, it's a little bit more serious. It would mean that Trip is planning something sinister in Algoma. If that is the case, finding out the formula will allow him to find an antidote. As far as he is concerned, the benefits of curing the victims outweigh any personal risk that he may face if he finds the formula. But, if it is indeed toxic, it is extremely important that he finds someone he can trust, someone who will not go and tell anyone else in case word gets back to Trip. Since he has no idea what is in it, he has decided that it's best to err on the safe side.

Who can he trust in Balavan with the skills and the discretion? It should not be anyone too close to town. In case the formula is dangerous, he wants to make sure that this person cannot accidentally let out his secret in a crowded place where there are ears everywhere. He also wants to avoid using a professor at a local university or a science teacher because they may want to know the source of this formula for future research or educational purposes. It has to be a humble and quiet person who keeps to him or herself and has little aspiration for glory. After pondering a little longer, Pete's eyes brighten.

"Ah, I know just the man," he mutters to himself as he makes his decision and makes his way to Balavan.

*

As Pete get close to town, he makes his way to the countryside. Taking a deep breath, he slows down. He has not been in this area in quite a while. When he was little, he would sometimes sneak out of the orphanage and wander the streets before anyone realized that he was missing. '

There were several times when he hitched a ride and ended up here. It's quiet and beautiful, especially at night when everyone else was asleep. It seemed like the whole world was his. There was nobody to tell him what to do, no one to make fun of him, and no rules to be followed. It was heaven.

He remembers it clearly. It seems the moon is always so much larger and brighter out here. He can always see the crater and the other freckles in the moon out here with his naked eyes. Next to it are hundreds, no hundreds of thousands of stars twinkling as if they are dancing to the sound of the crickets chirping and the frogs croaking. Down on the ground, the willow trees dance alongside it all as the wind gently blows on them creating the most comfortable breeze anywhere in the world. It is certainly more warm and welcome than the replica that he has created in the underground world of Algoma.

There is also something else that he always looks forward to when he is in this part of the countryside, the Sullivan Estate. When Pete was young, he would often wander to the property. He had always wished he could live in a place like this.

It's so big and beautiful, almost like a castle without the pretentiousness. The flowers around it attract the local birds and insects and almost seem to come alive. Being out in the middle of nowhere, he figured no one would catch him if he just went in for a peak. At first, he only dared to stay for a minute or two.

He would sneak into the garden and crouch down to smell everything, hoping to not be caught. Because he was always looking around to make sure that he was not seen, however, he would let his fear get the best of him, which really ruined the experience. After a while, he figured that no one was watching and began to stay longer with each trespass.

Of course, it is always when one lets down one's guard that they get caught. One day, he got braver and got a chance to sneak out when the sun was out.

144

As he snuck into the garden like he always did, he heard a gentle voice that said, "Hello, who are you?"

Startled, he looked up and saw a little boy about his age and stood up immediately. Like he is today, when he is taken by surprise, he is not capable of thinking up a lie.

Clearing his throat, he looks at the little boy's feet and mumbled, "Um, hi, um, my name is Pete."

The little boy looked at him with wide eyes and said, "Do you want to play?"

Dumbfounded, Pete didn't know what to say or think.

"Is this a trick?" Pete remembered asking himself.

No one had ever asked him that before. Pete had been the runt of the orphanage. He was sickly during his younger years, causing the other boys to shun him. Even when he finally got well enough to be able to go outside, they never asked him if he wanted to play with them. He always had to be the one to ask.

If he was lucky, they simply said no. If unlucky, he often was ridiculed or had things thrown at him. Worse, there were times when little boys would pretend to let him play with them, but ended up turning him into the butt of their joke as soon as he thought he had found a friend.

Children can be so cruel sometimes. After being rejected more times than he cared to admit, he simply gave up. He had learned to be self-sufficient. He had no need for a friend or a playmate, not even in imaginary one.

But, this boy was different. He looked very sincere in his request. He didn't look like he had a secret agenda, but what did he know? He was only about eight years old.

"Did cat catch your tongue?" the little boy asked curiously as he laughs.

Even though the little boy was laughing, it wasn't mean spirited like the ones he often endured in the orphanage. Instead, it was light hearted, which was strange to Pete.

He did not know what it was like to be teased in a friendly way, only ridiculed. At the time, he did not know the difference. He just knew that he was not upset but did not understand why.

"Huh?" Pete replied as he stared at the boy and decided to take the chance.

"What do I have to lose?" he had thought before saying, "Oh, um, sure, what would you like to play?"

"Cool!" the little boy said as he pulled him into his house.

Pete had never seen anything like it before. He didn't think it was possible, but the inside was more beautiful than the outside. There were marble columns and spiral staircases, just like in old movies, yet it did not scream extravagance.

The chandelier was elegant yet tasteful. The furniture looked handmade but stylish. There were no overpriced pieces of artwork or self-serving busts of themselves. Instead, there were fresh flowers and family portraits everywhere. Despite its large size, the home felt warm and welcome.

"By the way, I am Philip," the little boy said with a big grin.

Many years later, the little boy would become Max Sullivan's proud father, the renowned scientist. For now, he was just a little sweet child full of curiosity.

"Come on, I want you to meet my Mom and Dad. You will love them!"

At the invitation, Pete stopped and let go of his hand.

"What's wrong?" the little boy asked curiously.

"Do you mind if we keep this to ourselves?" Pete said.

Puzzled, the little boy doesn't understand why, but nodded and said, "OK" before leading his new friend to his room instead.

Being only one year apart from one another, they became fast friends, but for obvious reasons, however, Pete asked Philip to keep their friendship hidden from everyone else. For one thing, he was trespassing when he was supposed to be at the orphanage. If word got out where he had been hiding, his little escapades would end immediately. For another, since he usually could only sneak away at night, he did not want his new friend to get in trouble either.

When they got to Philip's room, Pete could not believe his eyes. There were toys everywhere from the floor to the wall and the ceilings. He remembers it as if it was yesterday.

There was a large fighter jet hanging from the ceiling. It was painted in the traditional army camouflage colors. There was not a brush stoke out of place. When he marveled at it, Pete remembers Philip proudly telling him that he and his father had made it together, spending hundreds of hours just to get it perfect.

Thinking back, that was probably what made Pete get started with his interest in aircrafts.

On the ground, there were other engineering marvels, albeit miniature versions. Like many boys of that age, he had a string of vehicles including fire engines, race cars, tanks, helicopters, and rockets, of every shape and size.

There were ones that did not move on their own and the ones that were controlled wirelessly. He personally favored the immobile ones, because those were the kind that he and Philip could play together, crashing into one another and laughing about them.

There were many times when they had to suppress their laughter in fear of being discovered by Philip's parents.

Now that he thinks about it, Pete is pretty sure that Philip's parents must have known that he was there because there were many nights when they were having so much fun that they were anything but quiet.

Yet, not once did they catch them. Perhaps, they felt sorry for the poor boy and pretended not to know about the intrusion.

Or, perhaps, they did not have the heart to interrupt knowing how happy their son was when he was with him. Although he had never formally met either one of them, he has seen them from afar and in pictures. There were times when he wished they were his parents.

Not once had he ever seen them angry at anything. Instead, the only image of them that he has is of a loving and smiling one.

When Philip grew up, Pete continued to keep his friendship with him a secret. He didn't really know why, but every time Philip had someone visit him, he would always excuse himself before their arrival. Perhaps, he always felt out of place as if he was unworthy of their company. Or, he was simply afraid that Philip's friends would ridicule him, much like the other boys in the orphanage did. Or, it could simply be a habit that both of them began to expect. It never bothered either one of them.

Then, their friendship began to fall apart when Philip fell in love with Sonya. It wasn't because Pete was jealous of her taking so much of his best friend's attention away from him.

It was much worse.

At first, it did not bother Pete that the two love birds were spending almost every minute of every day together.

Yes, it definitely took time away from his friend, but he didn't mind. Although he felt left out at times, he knew one day his friend was going to find a woman who would steal his heart.

In fact, he was happy for him. It was something he had hoped for himself, too. What he had not anticipated was that they would fall for the same woman.

Like with all of Philip's friends, Pete usually left before an introduction could be made. After knowing that Philip had fallen in love, however, Pete couldn't help but take a peek at his new girl. It didn't take him long to realize that it was a mistake.

He was immediately smitten by her the first time he caught a glimpse of her. She was the most beautiful woman he had ever seen, but he dared not let anyone know his true feelings. Instead, he decided to put a distance between himself and his best friend.

Before long, they had parted ways and he never had the guts to tell Philip why, which was a decision he would come to regret.

*

Before he knew it, he heard the horrible news that his dear friend and the woman of his dreams had been killed. When he first learned about their deaths, he was in utter disbelief. For about a minute, he stopped breathing as he felt his heart break into a million pieces. It wasn't until his subconscious kicked in to let him know that he was about to pass out did he snap out of it. He was so distraught that he stayed away from Balavan since their deaths.

He only came out of his surreal state of depression when he learned that they have a surviving son Max, who looks and acts every bit like his father, down to his fondness for vehicles and science.

Ever since then, he has been watching Max from a distance every chance he gets. Yes, it sounds creepy, but he sees it as a duty. In a way, he feels like he owes it to his best friend to watch over their pride and joy now that he is also an orphan.

Even though he is already 19 years old and attends the university, Pete still considers him a child who needs protection. Instead of coming out in the open and letting the young man know his identity and intentions, however, he prefers to remain in the shadows until now. Even though he has been to their estate many times, this is the first time he has come out in the open to the front door.

Ringing the door bell, he stands there silently awaiting the young man to appear. It seems to be an eternity before he hears the footsteps on the other side of the door approaching.

"Yes, may I help you?" Max asks as he opens the door.

"Hi, you don't know me, but my name is Pete. I was a friend of your father Philip."

Upon hearing his relation, Max shows a saddened smile as he says, "Please, would you like to come in?"

Nodding, Pete says, "Yes, thank you."

He has not stepped foot inside this home in over 20 years. It's like a homecoming for him. He considers Philip's home his home more than anywhere else he has ever lived in even though he has never actually lived here. He remembers every room the way it was decades ago. The marble columns are as shiny and pristine as the day he first laid eyes on them. Many of the portraits of Philip and his fathers are still hanging prominently on the walls. There are new ones with Max and his parents hanging next to them.

He is sad to see their pictures – so happy and vibrant, knowing that he will never see them alive again. The fresh flowers are no longer there, which dampers the mood even more.

"Are you alright?" Max asks.

"Yes, why do you ask?" Pete replies with a feigned smile, not realizing that there is a single tear in the corner of his right eye.

Not to embarrass his guest, Max walks with Pete towards the living room as he replies, "Oh, nothing. Don't worry about it. So, tell me. How do you know my father?"

Although he has never told anyone else about his friendship with Philip, he spares no details when telling it to Max as if he is giving his last rites to the priest. Pete even tells the young man about his affections for his mother, which makes Max somewhat uncomfortable. Who wants to hear about a love triangle between your parents and an old friend, especially after his parents have already deceased?

After Pete is done, Max says, "Why are you telling me all of this?"

"I want you to see me as family."

Surprised by the statement, Max says, "I don't know what to say."

"You don't have to say anything. I know you are still trying to digest what I have just told you. It's a lot to take in."

Max is not sure what to make of it. His brain tells him not to believe this man, but his gut tells him otherwise. He has never seen this man before in his life and has never read about him anywhere or heard anyone speak of him before either. Since his parents both kept meticulous records of their lives in their journals, he figures his father must have mentioned him sometime, somewhere before, but he cannot think of any entry that may have referred to this mysterious friend of his. Then again, his father is fiercely loyal. If they made a pact not to talk about their friendship, it's entirely possible that he would have left him out of all written records.

After a moment of silence, Max says, "Oh, where are my manners. Would you like something to eat or drink? I forgot to offer it to you earlier. It's almost dinner time. You must be hungry."

"Sure, I will take whatever you have."

"Do you have any special requests?"

Smiling, he has never considered Philip to be a chef. He wonders what kind of cook his son has turned out to be. Perhaps, he has learned a thing of two about the culinary arts from his lovely mother.

"No, whatever you are want is fine. I eat just about anything edible. I am not picky," Pete replies modestly.

"Oh, good. I don't have guests often. So, I don't have much to work with."

With that said, Max fires up the grill and makes a delectable rack of beef ribs.

"Need any help?" Pete asks as he begins to feel a little useless just sitting there waiting for his food.

"Sure. If you want, you can make the salad."

"No problem. I can do that."

As Pete leans over the sink to wash his hands before becoming the sous chef in Max's kitchen, he feels the bottle in his pocket. This place has brought back so many memories that he almost forgot what his original intention for coming here was. Taking out the bottle carefully, he places it on the kitchen counter before resuming the new task at hand.

During dinner, they continue to chat with one another about the past. As Max tells him about his childhood and his best friend Thom, Pete tells him about being the engineer who is rebuilding Algoma, but the topic of Amelia never arises. They are both fascinated with the other's tales. By the end of dinner, Max feels as if he knows Pete already and is starting to feel very comfortable with his father's old friend. As he is clearing the table, however, he sees the black bottle on the counter.

"What is that?" Max asks suspiciously as his joyous mood dampers.

Max remembers seeing that black bottle before. Even though there is no label, he is fairly certain it is the same as the one he has seen in the headquarters of the Desiderios. How can he forget? It's very hard to miss since Trip would not touch anything else besides that during dinner. At the time, he thought Trip was just not hungry and simply wanted to have a cold one during meal time. Now that Pete has it in his possession, he is starting to wonder what it is. Why does this supposed old friend of his father's have it? He never once mentioned knowing Trip or having any involvement with the Desiderios. What is he trying to pull?

"Oh, sorry. I was going to get the contents analyzed. Do you know anyone who can help me?" Pete asks without thinking.

At the moment, Max gets a sinking feeling in his gut.

"This guy is definitely playing me. Even if he doesn't know that I am a chemist, he must know that my father was, if he was indeed a friend of his." Max concludes.

"Not at the moment," Max replies coldly as he focuses his gaze on this man.

Although Pete senses that the conversation turning south, he has not recognized his mistake yet.

Puzzled, he asks, "Did I say something to offend you?"

"No, it's getting late. I have a long day tomorrow."

Pete knows that is the universal language for: "Please get out of my house now. You have overstayed your welcome."

Not wanting to press any further for the day, he simply says, "Thank you so much for your hospitality. We should do this again soon."

Giving a polite, but forced smile, Max simply nods before showing him the door.

*

Only after being escorted out of the house does Pete realize what he has done. He feels absolutely horrible. After all of this time, he has considered Max to be his adopted son. He has wanted their first meeting to be perfect, but botched it so badly in an instant. It certainly started out well. He has not had a conversation this relaxed with anyone in a very long time. Even when he is with Amelia, the discussions are usually a lot more formal. There always seems to be a distance between the two of them.

Why did he not put that stupid bottle away when he had the chance? How can he be so careless? There is simply no excuse, especially when the content of the bottle is in question. This is definitely no way to build a positive relationship with the boy. He knows he must amend it, and do so quickly.

The longer he waits, the longer Max's anger will build and the harder it will be to patch things up. He will never forgive himself if Max ends up hating him.

But first, he needs to give him enough time to settle down and cool off. He knows Max is a reasonable person. Once his initial emotional reaction subsides, he will come back and ask for clarification. He knows he is the type of person who will because his father certainly would. Judging from how similar father and son are, Max must have questions for him and would not let him get away without having them answered.

For now, he needs to step back and get a moment of peace and quiet to himself. At least, he has started the communication between the two of them.

It's *something* even if it's not what he has expected. As he leaves the main house, Pete is drawn towards a different part of property. Before he realizes it, he has wandered into the garden instead of leaving the property. Soon, he spots the same spot that he used to lie in when he was a child. It's been a long time, but it certainly doesn't feel like it. As he lies down, he began to feel remorse. He feels like he has let his friend down. Fidgeting, he sits back up. As he gazes in front of him, he realizes that he is only a few feet away from Philip and Sonya's final resting place. He can see the top of their gravestones over the tall grass.

Apparently, it has been quite some time since Max has been to see his parents. The thought saddens Pete. Perhaps, he has been preoccupied by other more important matters, like a major exam or something like that.

"Even so, is it so hard to find a few minutes to pay your respects?" Pete mumbles angrily.

Kneeling down, Pete starts clearing the weeds with his bare hands.

When he is done, he walks up to the gravestones and says, "Hello, old friend. It's been a long time."

Then, he lies down on the ground and stares into the sky before saying, "I hope you are enjoying your time up there with your lovely wife. I miss the old times. Even though they were some of the worst times in my life, you certainly made them better. I will always thank you for that."

After a pause, he says, "I want you to know that you two have brought up a wonderful boy. Like it or not, he is built just like you, my friend. Smart and courteous, too."

Then, he smiles and continues, "Probably got that from his mother. Hehe."

Closing his eyes, he tries to find the next words. Even though his friend is long dead, he still doesn't know how to break the news to him. It's as if he is speaking to him face to face.

Taking a deep breath, he opens his eyes and finally says, "But I have to confess. I think I messed things up with him. I came to visit him with the intention of creating a lasting relationship, but I screwed it up by mixing it with business. I didn't mean to, but I think he is really angry at me right now. What do you think I should do? I am really lost. I wish you were still here to give me advice, like you used to."

Chapter 12: Uncomfortable Alliance

As Pete stares into air pondering what to do, he hears footsteps. Alarmed, he gets up. He sees Max walking towards him.

Dusting himself off, Pete looks sheepish as he says, "I am sorry. I didn't mean to loiter at your home. I am leaving now. Thanks again for your hospitality."

"So, is it true?" Max asks.

"Is what true?" Pete asks curiously.

"Everything you said to my Dad?"

Blinking his eyes in shock, Pete did not realize that he was loud enough for anyone to hear. He certainly had not expected Max to be able to hear it all the way in the mansion.

"Yes," he finally answers. "Every word."

"So, why have you not come here before?"

From this question, Pete brightens up with optimism. For starters, he is given another chance to clear things up and he wants to make sure that he is going to do it right this time. He can tell that the conversation is about to pick back up, and better than before. During dinner, it was more of a casual dialogue to get to know one another. Now, it's on more deeper and more personal level.

Quietly, he says to himself, "Thanks, Philip!"

He knows his dear friend has heard him and has sent his son to give him a second chance. How else do you explain how Max just happens to know where he is? It's not like the garden is in direct view of the main house.

"But I have," Pete answers gently.

"When?" Max asks curiously.

"As often as I can, ever since your father died."

Max is taken aback by this revelation. Now that he mentions it, he has felt someone watching him before. It happens about once a month, but he never sees anyone. He has always discounted it as his imagination. On occasion, he thinks it's his parents coming back to make sure he is alright. On some days, it comforts him. On others, it creeps him out.

"Where?"

"I know it probably sounds really creepy, but sometimes, I watch you from over there," Pete says as he points towards a group of tall trees by the side of the main house. Then, he feels obligated to tell the whole truth and adds, "I have also been watching you at the University and at the market."

Shuddering, Max would be lying if he says that doesn't bother him. It actually does – quite a bit. It would bother just about anyone. Why wouldn't it? Some stranger he never knew existed before today has been watching him from his own property for months. In this case, it happens to be an old friend of his father's, but it could have been anyone.

Seeing that Max is getting quite uncomfortable, Pete tries to excuse it by saying, "but I only do so to make sure that you are safe. I owe it to your father to make sure that you are."

Even though he is still quite troubled, Max's brain tells him that Pete is sincere. No matter how eerie it may sound, he has good intentions.

"So, why haven't you introduced yourself until now?"

"I just never had the opportunity. The truth is I have never been very good with making friends, even with people I know. So, I always wait until the other person initiates the conversation first."

"Why is it different this time?"

"Because I also have a business proposition with you. I figure it's now or never."

"Ah, you mean the black bottle."

"Yes."

"How did you come upon it?"

Looking sheepish again, Pete admits, "I took it out of Trip's trash."

"Trash? Really?" Max asks with a light chuckle.

The fact that Max singles out the word *trash* rather than Trip's name is a good sign. He figures any normal person who has heard of Trip would automatically perk their ears at the sound of his name and be in awe. But, that doesn't seem to be the case here. It appears that Max knows the man and thinks that it's funny for someone to go through his garbage.

"Yes, I know. It's gross."

"And you put it on my counter?" Max says with a croaked smile and jokes, "Now, I have to disinfect it."

Seeing Max smile warms his heart. At least, he is on the right track even though he is starting to sound like a creepy and disgusting old fool with each passing minute.

"I am sorry. I will clean it for you."

"Oh, don't worry about it. I am just yanking your chain," Max says lightheartedly before asking, "So, why were you in Trip's trash?"

"Oh, oh," Pete grumbles to himself.

As usual, he has not thought ahead before opening his mouth. Of course Max is going to ask that question. Being a pacifist like his father, Max wants to believe everything Pete has told him and only asks questions that are directly related

159

to the conversation, like this one. If he has just left it alone, Max would not be the wiser. He seems to be perfectly content just talking about his father, until now, that is. It's like Pete has set himself up for an awkward moment.

Is he going to tell Max that he is suspicious of Trip? That in itself will surely raise more difficult questions considering that Trip is the current leader of Balavan. Even if he does, how is he going to start? Is he going to tell him about their conversation? That may not be the best idea since it has not been concluded. Last they spoke, Trip is still awaiting Pete's answer about the stockpile. It would be premature, not to mention irresponsible, to tell anyone else about the weapons repository. It can be blown out of proportion very quickly and cause pandemonium if not handled delicately. That is why he has not had the guts to finish the discussion with Trip. Letting Max in on it will just add another level of complexity that he rather not deal with.

Is he going to tell him about his alliance with Amelia? That would also be very uncomfortable considering that Victor is also responsible for the demise of Max's parents. Ugh, he dreads bringing that retched memory back up again. When Pete first found out about that little bit of detail, he was also quite distraught. By then, he has worked with Amelia for a decade and has come to respect her. Yet, Philip has always been *the* best friend. Even though Amelia did not pull the trigger, it tore him apart not to confront her about the Sullivans' death.

He wants to know why, but knows full well that she was and never has been her husband's keeper. Victor always did as he wished. No one, not even his beloved wife, can tell him what to do unless he also sees the merit in it. At least that is what he has convinced himself. That is the only way Pete can forgive Amelia for not stopping Philip's murder. If it takes that much effort for a friend to forgive her from the deed, how long would it take the victim's son to do the

160

same? The answer can very well be never. If Pete has to keep Amelia out of the picture, what else can he talk about? Drew? Simone? So far, he has not talked about his relationship with any of the Algomians. Maybe this is where he has to begin his tale. He doesn't see any other option, but still cannot find the words.

As the moment becomes even excruciatingly uncomfortable for him, Max comes to the rescue and says, "Wow, you are so obvious when you are speechless."

"Oh, I am sorry. You are right. I don't know what to say," Pete replies with a jaded smile.

"Well, I have never gone through anyone's garbage just because. You must been looking for something. Otherwise, that is a pretty disgusting habit," Max says as he twitches his nose.

"No, I assure you. It's not a habit," Pete replies before asking, "Can you have an open mind and reserve judgment until after I am done with the entire tale?"

"Of course," Max says without even thinking.

Taking a deep breath, Pete figures there is no point delaying the inevitable.

"You know about Trip's visit to Algoma."

"Yes, I have heard of it."

"Well, he was a little disappointed by what he saw."

"Really, I thought you said you helped to rebuild it as close to the original as possible."

"Yes, that is true, but what I didn't tell you is that it's a fortified version of it."

"By fortified, you mean there are armed guards everywhere?"

"Well, not quite."

161

As Pete describes the underground replica and the deep moat, Max's expression turns from amusement to concern.

"What happened?" Max asks in wonderment. "Why would they trap themselves in like that?"

"They don't see it as entrapment. They think of it as extreme protection."

"It sounds like they overcompensated."

"Yes, that much is for sure."

"OK, so what does that have to do with you digging in his trash?"

"I am going to come to that," Pete says as he tries to pace himself while still keeping control of the conversation. "Do you mind if we continue this conversation inside?"

"Sure."

Pete is glad to be able to take another breather as he gets up to return to the main house, but the break is to be short lived.

Like a little boy who is entrenched in a fairy tale of sorts, Max asks, "So, what did Trip do after he found out about the fortifications?"

"I don't know that for sure. I wasn't there when he first got there."

"Then how do you know that he was sorely disappointed?"

"Oh, oh, here it goes again," Pete laments to himself.

Clearing his throat, he says, "I spoke to him later and found out then."

"Ah, that makes sense," Max says as he nods his head.

"Whew, that was a good save!" Pete says to himself.

"How did the two of you meet?"

"By chance. We were looking for shade at the same place," Pete replies with tongue in cheek.

Yes, there is a certain amount of truth to that, but it's far from the whole truth, but he figures there is no harm in bending it a little. Besides, he isn't about to tell Max that he was snooping around first. It would make him look bad.

"Ah, so it's meant to be! Kind of like how you and my Dad met, right?" Max says excitedly.

"Well, I guess, but I wouldn't put it quite that way."

"Po-tay-toes, Po-tah-toes. What did you two talk about?"

"Well, let's just say that we didn't quite see eye-to-eye at first."

"Why not?"

"I guess we started on the wrong foot. We both know a little about the other from a mutual friend of ours, but we don't know enough. We kind of began to test one another to see if the other is lying."

"Oh, that's too bad."

"When we parted, we haven't quite mend the fences yet. You know, kind of like how we almost ended up last time we spoke," Pete says somewhat embarrassed.

"So, that just means that you need to have another conversation with Trip to clear things up!"

Pete figures this is as good of an opportunity as any to explain how he came upon the black bottle and says, "You may be right, but, as you probably know, he has quite an intimidating presence. I was a little afraid of the man, still am, actually. So, I decided to go to his house to see if I can find out something more about him without having to face him. Yes, it's a little cowardly and I feel bad about it. I really do, but I figure studying a person's living space is one of the best ways to get to know him."

"How did you get into his house in the first place?" Max asks dubiously as he thinks back to how Pete has admitted to spying on him secretly for months.

"I have the key."

"How do you have a key to Trip's home if you are not friends? Are you his landlord or something?"

"Please don't tell anyone this, but when I started rebuilding the town, there were many issues, especially being underground. To make it easier to fix the problems as quickly as possible, I had access to everyone's home. Since we are still building, I still have it."

Taken aback by the confession, Max says, "Isn't that called trespassing? I would think that betrays the trust of every one of the residents."

He knows it does, but he has never thought of it that way. Now that Max says it out loud, it sounds really bad, even to him.

"I only use it out of necessity."

"What did Trip do to make it a necessity?"

"I fear for the safety of the new Algoma."

"What evidence do you have that he plans on doing anything to the new Algoma?"

"I don't. It's just a gut feeling."

"I cannot believe you did that simply because of a feeling," Max says disappointingly.

"I usually trust my gut. It has kept me alive all this time and I am definitely no spring chick," Pete says as he laughs nervously trying to lighten up the mood.

"What did you find?" Max asks out of sheer curiosity.

Even though he knows what Pete did was wrong, he figures there is no harm asking about his findings if it's already done.

"The place was clean except for the bottle. I figure it has some kind of significance."

"Why would you say that?"

"It just seems odd that he would have such a clean place but leaving something personal like that. It's like he left it there for me to find."

"Hm," Max replies before tensing up and asking, "Have you ever entered my home before without my knowledge?"

"No."

Even though Max is glad to hear it, it doesn't make him feel any better. Once again, he has serious doubts about this man.

"Anyways, now that I have answered your question, will you help me?" Pete says with a crooked smile.

Max cannot believe the man is still asking him for help after admitting that he is a trespasser and quite possibly a thief. No matter how he justifies it, Pete comes across as nothing but a thug to him. After staring at him for another minute, he decides to give him a chance anyways, not because he thinks he deserves it, but because of his relationship with his father. If Philip can trust the man, he cannot be all bad, right? Who knows? He may be right. Trip may actually be planning something against Algoma. He doubts it, but he is a mysterious man. If he does, Max is pretty sure there is a very good reason for it.

"I will help you analyze the content of the bottle, but that is it," Max finally says as he crosses his arms.

"Thank you!" Pete says as he takes out the bottle and places it on the table.

Now that Pete has what he came for, Max figures he will excuse himself and leave. Instead, he continues to sit there and squirm.

"If there anything else you need?" Max asks.

"Well, I was hoping that we can get to know each other better."

"Why?"

Saddened at the question, Pete gets up and says, "I see you don't."

Realizing that he has his feelings, Max says, "No, no, please sit down."

"You know, I am serious when I said I want to make sure that you are safe. I swear that is the *only* reason I watch you. I am simply try to take care of you, and not to stalk you."

"I know, but I can take care of myself."

"I know you can, but I want you to know that I am here for you if you need me."

"Um, OK."

Although he knows very well that Max is far from being convinced, Pete has said his piece. There is no point lingering any longer.

He gets up and simply says, "Again, thank you," before heading out the door.

It's like déjà vu. Pete has screwed up again. He is pretty sure there is no way of winning Max over, ever, now that he has mess things up twice. This time, he keeps walking and heads for the hotel on Main Street. Even Philip would have a difficult time believing him by now.

"Is he for real?" he mutters to himself as he closes the door.

As he looks out the window, he can see Pete's drooping head as he walks off of the property. For a split second, he almost feels sorry for the man. Despite his forgiving nature, however, Max is not sure what to make of this latest guest. It seems he is genuine, but a genuine what – a genuine con artist or a genuine lost soul? He leans towards the latter, but the jury is still out on that.

*

For now, it doesn't matter. The only thing he has committed to do is to study Trip's bottle. Just like the fortification, it sounds like an overkill to want to analyze somebody's drink, or rather trash, but he is going to humor him anyways. Perhaps, that will give him a peace of mind and move on. Going into his, or rather his father's, lab, Max takes out his chemical analysis instrumentation and puts on his lab coat and goggles. Even though he is pretty sure there is nothing dangerous in bottle, he does it anyways, out of habit. Besides, that was what his father always did when he was in the lab. Putting on all of the gear makes him feel closer to Philip.

As Max starts to look at the ingredients, he immediately sees what he has expected, ingredients for a rich and nutritious meal. At first glance, it looks a lot like a breakfast smoothie with green leafy vegetables, egg proteins, legumes, fruits, herbs, and spices. There are also very potent vitamins and minerals mixed in it. Even though there are some unique looking vegetation in it, Max is starting to get bored within ten minutes of starting the analysis. As he often does when he is uninterested, he goes to the kitchen to fix himself a big juicy sandwich with the works and a bottle of icy cold beer.

As he munches on his snack and gulps down his drink loudly, he haphazardly looks under his instrumentation to see the results as if he is merely reading his junk mail or watching television. It's obvious that he is not paying any attention to what he is looking at. There are lots of numbers and colorful line charts overlapping one another. As he continues to click on various buttons to glance over the data quickly, however, he finds something he does not recognize. He immediately stops eating and dusts off the crumps on his pants.

Doing a double take, he wonders, "What in the world is that thing?"

Having been a chemist, albeit an unofficial one, for well over a decade, he recognizes chemical components of just about every known element in the world, but he does not know what he is looking at. Even the sophisticated instrumentation does not know what to make of it. It seems to be something that has never been recorded. Looking at it under a microscope, it looks like it is glowing.

Is it radioactive? Why in the world would Trip be drinking something like that? Wouldn't that kill him? It's like trying to drink mercury for immortality. Then, a thought comes to mind. What if this is an additive that Trip added afterwards to the bottle to make sure that no one drinks from it and lives to tell? No, that cannot be it. Trip is not that evil. If he is going to kill someone, he always has a target in mind. Doing something like that is not in his nature. For the next few hours, he tries to isolate the element to determine what it is. By day's end, he still has no clue.

He is amazed that a seemingly trivial task has become his new fascination. He is thankful that school is not in session right now. Otherwise, he would be in deep trouble with his professors. For the next few weeks, Max is consumed by the mysterious element in the potion. He has

168

done absolutely nothing but study it. He only takes a few hours of break to sleep and take a quick bite to eat. Because there is only a precious few drops left in the bottle, he tries to be ever so diligent in making sure he does not waste anything.

When he finally runs out of ideas, he goes to the University to do some research, combing through every experiment that he can find and every rare flower or mineral from the most remote corners of the world that he can find, hoping to discover a clue. Despite his exhaustion, Max continues his quest to find out what this mystery element is.

Chapter 13: Unforeseen Detour

Max doesn't even realize how pale and thin he has gotten over the last month. Feeling a little drained, he decides to get a cup of coffee from the local shop. As he sips his drink, he hears a familiar voice.

"Hello, Max."

Turning around, Max says, "What are you doing here?"

It's Pete. For the past month, he has been waiting patiently for the result of the potion. Because of the guilt that he has been feeling since they last spoke, he has been too ashamed to show his face to the young man. It is entirely by coincidence that he meets him there. He has to muster all the courage he can find to get himself to talk to him.

"Getting a cup of my favorite latte. I wasn't following you, I swear." Pete says with a smile.

Max is so tired that he doesn't care even if Pete is stalking him.

"Are you OK?" Pete asks with a concerned look.

"Yes, why do you ask?"

"Well, you look like you lost about ten pounds since the last time I saw you and your eyes are red and sunken in."

"Gee, thanks. You look great, too," Max replies with a heavy dose of sarcasm.

Smiling, Pete knows that Max doesn't mean anything by his comment. Over the years, he has encountered many seemingly nice people who have said rude things when they are not themselves. He can clearly tell that is the case with Max. Besides, he figures he still owes the young man for having alienated him during their last two meetings. The least he can do is to tolerate a couple of sly remarks.

"If you are not busy, do you want to grab something to eat? My treat," Pete says.

At the sound of the word eat, Max's stomach instantaneously growled, forcing a smile on his face.

"Why not? You heard the boss," Max says referring to his gut. "I think it's time to put something in there."

As they go to the nearest burger joint, the two men enjoy their meal talking about nothing but the weather and how beautiful summer is in Balavan. Both men know that there is an elephant in the room, but nobody is willing to start. Pete obviously does not want to start because the last time he did, he made a mess of things. He figures since Max is a renowned member of the chemist community, he must have figured out the components of Trip's bottle by now. Based on his reputation, it should take no more than a couple of hours for someone as well versed in analyzing the elements as he is.

Yet, at the same time, he is worried about the answer. If it's nothing serious, why is Max not bringing up the subject? A part of him is wondering if it is indeed a secret poison or, worse.

Judging from the fact that Max is totally out of shape, he was probably right about suspecting that bottle. The more he thinks about it, the more he becomes anxious.

Meanwhile, Max does not want to start because he is trying to avoid having to talk about the mystery element that he is unable to identify. In addition to making him look bad, it would raise more questions than he can answer.

If he so much as brings up the subject, Pete is sure to want to ask for details. Considering how he is more analytical than tactical, Max does not want to ruin a wonder and relaxing meal by having Pete say the wrong things.

No matter how much the two want to stay away from the topic, however, a little bit of it comes out when Max asks, "So, how is life treating you?"

"Oh, good. I have been trying to replicate some of the local flowers of Algoma, but not having any success. What about yourself?"

Although Pete means nothing by it, Max sees it as a teaser to start talking about his findings. After all, replicating a plant requires the usage of a laboratory and the understanding of its components. If this were any other conversation with anyone else, he would have offered to help or at least ask what kind of problem he is having.

Knowing his audience, however, he is going to stay as far away from that line of conversation as possible.

"Oh, everything is cool," Max replies casually, trying to end the conversation before it really starts.

Unfortunately, Pete does not get the hint and continues, "There is this one very rare flower. It blooms only at night. You should see it. It's absolutely beautiful."

"I am sure it is," Max replies nonchalantly, hoping that by sounding disinterested, Pete will drop it.

But, as expected, he doesn't as he continues, "Its golden yellow and looks like it twinkles when it blooms."

"Twinkles?"

For some reason, that word pique Max's interest. Even though it may be a reach, he wonders if this is the item that he is looking for. All of this time, he has been looking for radioactive items. What if it's not radioactive at all, like this flower that Pete is talking about?

"Yes, from far away, it looks like it glows, almost like the stars in the sky. The problem is it needs a certain amount of ultraviolet light to grow and in our underground city; we try not to recreate anything that may be harmful to

172

humans. And, even if the condition is perfect, it's difficult to grow, making my job that much more difficult. But, I got to tell you, it will definitely be worth it when I manage to get it to work!"

Out of curiosity, Max says, "It does sound quite exquisite. What is it called?

"Oh, there is no translation. It's a rare beauty that only grows in Algoma. I couldn't begin to tell you what it's called."

"Where can I find one?"

"I have it at the hotel if you want to take a look."

"Sure!"

Smiling, Pete is glad that Max is interested in something that he is working on. As far as he is concerned, it's definitely a good sign. Maybe they can forge a friendship based on common interest.

As soon as Max sees the flower, he knows there is something special there.

"That must be it. That must be the mystery element in the potion!" Max exclaims to himself in his head.

"It's so beautiful. Do you mind if I take a petal?"

"Not at all! Help yourself! There is plenty more where it comes from." Pete replies joyously.

He is not about to refuse the man anything at this point. Even if he asks for his kidney, he probably would give it to him without any hesitation. Just like the last time they spoke, there is an awkward moment of silence, but the table has turned. It is now Max who is stilling in Pete's room and not leaving even though he has gotten what he originally came to get.

"So, why the interest in the flower?" Pete asks innocently to break the silence.

"The way you tell it, it sounds so exquisite. I just have to see it for myself. I have to say I am not disappointed."

Then, there is another moment of silence.

Smiling, Pete says, "Is there anything else I can help you with?"

Even though he really wants Pete to take him to the field where these flowers grow so he can get a better idea of their anatomy, condition, etc, Max is not sure if he should. While he wants to know as much about it as possible, he wonders if he should leave know before Pete wonders why.

Yet, without a name, it's nearly impossible to find anything on it in his research. Then, his cautious side tells him that it's better to be safe than sorry. Since he already has a sample, he may be able to find enough data from what he already has.

"No, that's fine. It's my turn to thank you for your hospitality," Max says with a big smile.

Pete returns the gesture and offers to shake his hand, which Max takes. Happy that everything seems to be going well, Pete says, "We should do this again soon!" exactly the same way Max said it last time.

The inside joke is not lost on Max. He smiles and says, "Touché!"

*

As Max heads back to his house, he is excited about his new lead and wants to get back as quickly as he can. Normally, he takes the metro bus when he heads to the University, but since he does not want to waste a single minute waiting for the next one to show up, he opts to take the taxi instead.

174

It will be a mistake he will regret very quickly. His eagerness to discover the new element has led him to become completely unaware of his surroundings or where the driver is taking him. Knowing that the ride will be fairly long, he is not paying any attention to where the taxi is going.

For over twenty minutes, he is staring at the flower petal closely. Not once has he looked out of the window to check the route. By the time he bothers to look up, he has no idea where he is. All he sees is an open road with a lot of trees. There are no road signs anywhere, but since it is still a paved road, he figures they are still heading in the right direction. Giving the driver the benefit of the doubt, he figures he is simply taking an alternate route home. Nevertheless, knowing that taxi drivers get paid by the mile in these parts, he is suspecting that he may be taking a longer route so he can charge him more.

Just to be sure, he opens the hole in the divider between him and the driver and jokingly says, "Driver, you are not just taking me for a ride, are you?"

The driver simply keeps quiet and continues to drive.

Somewhat annoyed by the lack of response, Max says a little louder, "Where are we? Are we almost there?"

Again, the driver disregards him. He is not even looking back to acknowledge the fact that his passenger has asked him a question.

"Is he deaf?" Max asks himself.

No, he cannot be. He answered when he first got in the taxi to tell him where he was heading. It would be very difficult for a deaf man to do his job. He knows he is loud enough to be heard. It's not like there is a lot of traffic noise that can muffle his voice. That means the driver is simply ignoring him on purpose.

After making his conclusion, he becomes angry and says, "What is wrong with you? I asked you a question!"

Still not getting a response, he knocks on the divider and says, "Stop, driver. I am getting off right here."

Again, the driver keeps going without acknowledging him. Starting to panic, Max is starting to get scared.

"What is going on? Am I being kidnapped?" He says to himself.

Looking out the window, nothing has changed. They are still going on the same deserted road.

"Driver, if you don't stop now, I am calling the police!" Max threatens.

He reaches into his pocket for his phone to make good his threat, but there is no signal. In this day and age, that never happens unless there was absolutely no civilization anywhere.

The only reason why there would be no signal is if the taxi has a signal blocker on it. If it does, he is sure he has been kidnapped. He figures he has no choice but to try to open the door of the taxi cab and roll out. He has seen people do it before on television, but has never attempted something that dangerous before in his life. He is terrified that he may end up killing himself, but figures he has no other choice. He has heard all of the horror stories of a kidnapping. Once you are in the vehicle, you are as good as dead unless you find a way out. He, for one, has no intention of being a statistic.

Taking a deep breath, he reaches for the door handle with his right hand as he gets ready to open the lock with his left. Closing his eyes for a second, he gathers the nerves to do it.

"One, two, three!" he mentally counts before yanking the door lock to the open position while pushing the handle at the same time.

To his horror, or relief, depending on which part of him you ask, the door does not budge. More than ever, he knows he is trapped. There is nothing left to loose. He puts his foot up the window to try to kick it out.

"Bong!" the window makes a resonant sound. It seems to be bullet proof.

This is no ordinary kidnapping. Whoever is taking him has made all of the measures necessary to prevent an escape and it cannot be easy or cheap.

"Think! What else can I do to get out of this?" Max says to himself as he hits the side of his head.

There is one more thing, but it's risky. Then, again, so is jumping out of a moving vehicle that is going about seventy miles an hour. Squeezing both hands through the small hole in the divider, he tries to choke the driver. While the attempt can be applauded, the execution cannot. It actually looks kind of comical. The hole is not big enough for him to push both of his arms through. He can only reach the driver's neck with the tips of his fingers.

Instead of grabbing his neck, Max ends up tickling him, which startles the driver as he swerves a little before returning to his emotionless self. It's apparent that he has not expected to get touched like that. There is no point trying again with only one arm since he cannot wrap it around the driver's neck. He can scratch him or pull his hair, but what would that accomplish besides a very angry driver.

Removing his arms, Max sticks his face up to the hole in the divider and screams, "You better stop now or you are SOOOO going to regret it!!!"

Yes, it's an empty threat. Max knows it and so does the driver. By now, Max is huffing and puffing in anger, so much so that he is no longer scared. Like a little boy who is grounded, Max leans back with his arms crossed seething and not knowing what to do. He is out of options. He cannot break his way out of here and has no way of stopping the man.

"What would Thom do?" Max asks himself.

Thom can always get out of the stickiest situation. When they were young, there was no teacher, parent, or any figure of authority who could keep him in anywhere if he doesn't want to. He has crawled out of dozens of windows, climbed up and down gutters and lattices, hung over numerous balconies, and jumped down plenty of tall structures.

He never seemed to hurt himself no matter how reckless it looked. Since Thom has never been trapped in a moving vehicle before, Max has no idea what else he may have done, but one thing is for sure, he would never just sit there and sulk.

Putting his face back up to the hole in the divider, he studies the front of the taxi to see if there is anything he can do to stop it. It has the usual things in any car, the instrument panel, the glove compartment, the steering wheel, the Global Positioning System.

"That's it!" Max says to himself.

Even though the GPS is not turned on, maybe he can turn it on and send a distress call from it. Maybe, they will send a squad car to check on the taxi. Looking into his backpack, he looks for something he can use to hit the button on the GPS panel. He sees his phone, a water bottle, the flower petal, a couple of pens, a rubber band. Perfect! Since Max is an excellent shooter, it should be able to use the rubber band to hit the target. Making sure that the driver is not looking, he takes his aim. Just as he is about to release it from his finger, the taxi takes a sharp turn to the left, knocking him back. As he tries to sit back up, he realizes that he has lost the rubber band. Since it was in the locked position in his fingers, it shot off into the hole in the divider and has landed squarely on the gear shift lever.

"Ugh! Just perfect! Can this day get any worse?!?" Max exclaims in frustration.

There, he said it. Those infamous words that make sure that, yes, things will get worse. As he continues to try to find ways to get out, he suddenly realizes that the taxi is slowing down. He looks out the window; it's still a bunch of trees.

"Oh, no. Where am I?" Max laments as he starts to panic.

In the middle of nowhere, the taxi stops. A menacing looking man holding a high powered rifle with a ski mask over his face and camouflage uniform, complete with heavy army boots, calmly comes out of the trees.

"Oh, no! Is he going to kill me?" Max panics as he holds on to the door.

Even though his life may be on the line, his thoughts turn towards the flower petal. He knows that once the man grabs him out of the taxi cab, he is going to lose his back pack and all of its contents. He needs to save his precious find before it disappears forever. He carefully tucks it into his shirt pocket. If he makes it out alive, at least it will not be for nothing.

Swinging the door wide open, the man says, "Let's go."

Grabbing his back pack, Max dutifully complies with the order. As expected, the man takes the back pack away from him and throws to into the woods. Even though he is in no position to lecture, he just has to say it. It's one of pet peeves – rude people. He just cannot stand them.

"Hey, that's just uncalled for!" Max exclaims.

He knows he is going to regret doing it, but before he actually does, the man hits him squarely in the back with the rifle and shouts, "Keep moving!"

It instantly knocks him to the ground. It hurts so much that he loses his breath from it, but he knows he must stand up and comply. If he doesn't, he is sure to get hit again. Even though the first strike already hurts, he knows it's going to be that much worse the second time. He knows his captor's type.

They are cold and ruthless. They have to be to be in their line of work. Their employers cannot risk using a man who may be swayed by sympathy or feelings of any kind besides the joy of inflicting sheer pain.

Before he gets very far, Max sees another man with a similar outfit and rifle as his captor come out of the trees towards the taxi cab. Half expecting him to double cross the driver and shoot him in the head instead of paying him for his services, Max freezes for a second. Of course, this invokes another jab in the back.

Thankfully, this one is slightly less painful since he is still aching terribly from his first injury. Before he can get up from the second hit, the taxi driver speeds back towards the direction that they came from, and the second captor catches up to them. It seems his captors have kept their end of the bargain.

"Oh, great. Now, I have to deal with both of them," Max laments.

Despite the extremely dismal look of things, it's not all bad. Being a pacifist, he often tries to see the good side of people, even his captors. The fact that the taxi driver lives

180

means that they cannot be *all* bad. They must simply be following orders.

Since he has not done anything horrible to anyone, he is hoping that they have no plans on killing him. He just needs to cooperate. While the thought is somewhat comforting, he is hoping that whatever they want from him, he is able to provide.

For the life of him, he cannot figure out what they may want from him. The only thing he can think of is ransom money, but he really doesn't have that much money to warrant such an elaborate plot. Although his parents have left him a sizeable property, they have not left him much liquid asset.

In fact, after paying for his tuition and expenses, he doesn't really have very much left for anything else. Besides, judging from their rifles, they mean business. If they want to target someone for ransom, it should be someone who has an obvious amount of it, and that certainly is not him.

So, if not money, what else can they possibly want? His is just a student who nothing much of value. The only other things he can think of are his friends. Can they be after one of them – Thom, perhaps? Or, maybe they are aiming higher.

Since he was a part of the Desiderios, can they be after Trip himself? Although it's a stretch, it *is* possible since he is the only one of Trip's circle who lives way out in the middle of nowhere. Everyone else may be more difficult to entrap. As he continues to ponder, they reach a small portable building hiding amongst the trees that looks old and dingy.

"Oh, no, am I to be kept there? It's disgusting," Max begrudges again.

The first captor reaches for the door and opens it. At first Max is surprised that it is not even locked, but it passes quickly.

"Of course, it's so bad that even they don't care if anyone steals it," Max thinks sarcastically.

As soon as he enters inside, Max takes a sigh of relief. It looks much better on the inside than out. It seems the dismal exterior is nothing but a ruse to deter any curious onlookers who may happen to come by here, wherever *here* is. Based on what he has seen, he is a long way from Balavan. He was in the taxi for a good hour before they stopped.

During the time he bothered to look out the window, he did not see a single car on the road from either direction, which he finds strange. Normally, a nice and relatively wide road like this is well traveled. Of course, that is the least of his concerns right now. He needs to focus on what is going to happen to him.

Turning his attention back to the inside of the small building, he sees four white walls, which smell freshly painted. The floor is completely covered in granite tiles, which seems to be overkill for an interrogation room, but he is not going to question that for the moment.

Continuing his gaze, he sees a simply but stylish wicker armchair in the middle of the room. Against the wall are two matching armchairs. In between them is a camera, which is to be expected for a kidnapping. How else can they get a proof of life?

What strikes him as interesting is that it is not just *any* camera, but a professional grade one that is typically used in production companies or newsrooms. It seems the kidnappers want to capture every detail and emotion in this interrogation. Are they planning on torturing him and filming every gash, blood, and tears on film? The thought gives Max the creeps. It is better not to speculate on it too much or he is going to lose his nerve and give up too easily.

Focusing his attention to the four corners of the building, he sees elegant busts of Greek gods or goddesses standing on marble columns. The two in the front of the building are Zeus and his wife Hera, the power couple. The other two are Hermes and Apollo, the artist and intellectual. Somehow, it almost seems the selected statues and their positions have meaning.

Those in the front, namely the interrogators, are the powerful deities who have final say on the outcome of this session as if they are the judges in a trial. Meanwhile, those being interrogated in the back are the ones with the knowledge that they seek. That thought relaxes him a little bit.

Contrary to the previous scenario, this one seems to suggest that the interrogation is purely for informational purposes. If he cooperates, he may get out of it unscathed.

Regardless of what is really going to happen, one thing is for sure. He finds it very interesting that the brain behind this little scheme seems to have an exquisite taste in decoration and a fondness for mythology. Why would someone go through that much expense for a little shack in the forest just to kidnap someone? Whoever is behind it obviously has money and appears to be a patron of the arts. That certainly rules out the theory that he is being captured for ransom. It sounds like this person has money to burn, which is certainly not the case with him.

Who can it be? There is only one person he knows in this entire Dominion with that kind of cash to throw around – Thom Richardson, his best friend.

After the Six Year War, many people lost their homes and everything they own. Thom, on the other hand, has inherited his father's fortune, which effectively makes him the richest man in Balavan.

"No, it cannot be him," Max thinks to himself.

Despite his sudden wealth, he is more of an athletic person. He can care less about art and history. In fact, he may not even know, or care, that those busts are Greek. As far as he is concerned, it's a statue of some guy or gal. If it's not him, who else can it be? After thinking for a second, another name comes to mind – his mother Amelia. Even though she has to part with Victor's fortune, it's no secret that she still has a lot of her own stashed away. She certainly has a fondness for fine arts. He remembers she used to have a very fine art collection in her home.

If it is her, the question is why? Why in the world would the mother of his best friend want to kidnap him? The thought is almost absurd. Even though she was never the motherly type, she still liked him, at least he thought. She has never been mean to him nor ever yelled at him, even when he knew that he and Thom were not being the best of boys. Then again, she may be upset with him because he was a part of the Desiderios who took down her beloved husband.

Chapter 14: The Interrogation

Before Max can consider other potential kidnappers, one of the captors barks, "Sit!"

Max complies immediately.

"What was your business with the man in the coffee shop?"

It seems the interrogation has started and these two are going to do it. Is it just the two of them? It cannot be. They both look way too brutish to appreciate the finer things in life.

"Answer the man!" the second man barks as he punches him in the jaw.

Shocked, Max has not expected that. They seem to be playing a game of good cop bad copy and the bad thing is the cold one asking the questions seems to be the good cop. He felt his sore jaw and glares at the ground. They didn't have to punch him to get the message across.

"I... I was having coffee."

Not convinced, the first man repeats his question, "What were you doing with him?"

"I am telling the truth! I was having coffee and he happened to be there at the same time. So, we drank coffee."

Seeing him nod to the second man, Max knows exactly what that means as he mutters, "Oh, oh."

Before he knows it, the fist is back on his face.

"Ow!" Max screams.

It's really starting to hurt and it's only been less than a minute. Being a sharpshooter, he has never had to come in close contact with the enemy before. Being a pacifist, he also never had the misfortune of being in a physical fight with anyone before.

Hence, being socked in the face is a new thing to him. He is surprised at how much it actually hurts. They make it look so easy on movies where people would bleed everywhere, but still have the energy to smart mouth their captors.

"What do they want from me?" Max asks himself.

By now, he genuinely has no idea what they are asking. Like people often do when they are in a state of emergency, Max is panicking and his brain is going blank. All he can think of is the coffee and idle chatter. Since it just happened, he can almost play it out minute by minute from where he first saw Pete to how much his latte cost. With each strike, Max spills out more details of their meeting, but that only angers his captors more.

It's like having a teacher ask you a question in class. Even though you are sure you have answered it correctly, she keeps rephrasing it, expecting you to give her a different answer.

He honestly has no idea what else these men think he and Pete were doing in there. Of course, what he doesn't realize is that his captors don't literally mean what he and Pete were doing when they were physically sitting there.

What they really want to know is whether or not Pete and he are involved in a secret mission and what they may be plotting.

The interrogation keeps going like that for another hour. By then, Max's face is bruised and his spirit is gone. Even the captors are getting tired of hitting him. They both decide to take a break.

Taking a cigarette out of his pocket, one of the captors says to the other, "Want one?" as if they are just two friends on a break.

The second man nods as they both go outside to take a smoke while Max takes a sigh of relief as he sinks into the chair wondering what in the world has he gotten himself into. Every part of his body aches.

They were ruthless with their hits. There was no part of his body that didn't ache in pain.

There is also blood splatters all over the floor in front of him. Despite the pain, he tries to stand up, half expecting to fall. Besides a slight wobbling, he is able to get up with no problems. Smiling, he is that nothing seems to be broken. Even though his legs are purple and blue with swelling already starting, they will heal in time.

With his swollen eyes, he tries to open them to see if there is any way he can escape while his captors are otherwise occupied. Although the marble busts are still there in its pristine condition, he no longer sees them as such. Instead, the room is not nearly as beautiful as it was when he first entered it. Now, it is filled with anguish and disgust.

Shuddering, Max tries to concentrate on what may be useful. He knows he doesn't have much time. Since there is only one door with no windows, he cannot very well sneak out of another exit.

Being much smaller and weaker than either one of his captors, he has little chance of out running them, either. Hence, he needs to find something else that he can use, a weapon or something. Alas, there isn't any. The only thing they used is their fists and their feet. So far, it doesn't look like they intend on killing him even though there were moments during the past hour, the longest he has *ever* endured in his life bar none, when he was sure he was going to die.

Then, he looks next at one of the captors' armchairs. There are two bottles of beer sitting on the floor, both of which are half drunk.

The floor has a ring of water where the cold dew from the bottles has gathered. Although he has not drunk anything since his capture, he has no intention of sharing a beer with his captors. Looking into the chair, he notices that there is something that slid towards the back of the cushion. Curious, he walks closer to see what it is. It is the answer that he has been waiting for – a phone.

Instead of calling the police, however, his first instinct is to call his best friend Thom. Even though, for a brief moment, he had thought that his friend may be the one responsible for his kidnapping, he is dialing his number without a second thought. After the first ring, there is no answer.

"Come on! Come on!" Max begs.

Before the second ring finishes, he hears a familiar voice, "Hello? Who's this?"

Max has never been so happy to hear his friend's voice.

"Thom," Max whispers. "It's me, Max. Please help me. I have been kidnapped, but I don't know where I am."

"What? Who's this? Speak up." Thom says in a muffled voice.

Max's heart just sinks into his gut. The signal must be jammed, for him not to be able to hear him at all. His captors have done their homework, which is probably why they have no problem leaving something as important as a phone here unsupervised with their prisoner.

"Oh, no!" Max panics.

For a second, he wonders if the phone is actually a trap, left to see who he would call, perhaps leading them to Trip or whoever their intended target is. Then, he hears his captors' voice get just a little bit louder. He knows he is out of time and puts the phone back in the cushion exactly where he found it and returns to his chair to sulk. As soon as he sits back down, the door opens.

"Are you ready to tell us what we want to hear yet?" the captor says with a cold and booming voice.

Now that he has rested a little, Max's brain has returned to him. Suddenly, he realizes what it is that they have been asking all of this time. They want to know about his analysis of Trip's bottle. That must be the business between Pete and him that they want to know.

But, why? Who are these people? How do they even know what he has agreed to do for Pete? Neither one of them ever mentioned it during the day, at least not directly.

That can only mean one thing: they have been following them. It's another troubling thought, but he doesn't have the time to be concerned about that right now. Instead, he needs to figure out what he needs to say before getting hit again. Should he tell them what he is working on?

Every fiber of his being tells him no – not just no, but not in a million years no. There is no telling what these thugs are going to do with this information. All he knows is that they are bad people and from his experience, people like them can use any news against their targets. He cannot risk it.

Then again, what is he going to say? He has no clue. To top it off, he is a terrible liar. Even ruffians like them can tell if he is making it up.

As he braces for the interrogation to continue, he closes eyes and tries to minimize the impact of his captor's fist by imagining better days when there were no worries.

189

Those days long past when his loving parents were still with him and his friend Thom was true and innocent, completely void of any complications or worries. As his mind continues to wander, for a moment he actually has forgotten that he is still a prisoner.

Then, he realizes it must have been a whole minute since they have come back in, but they have not continued their walloping session. With his eyes still closed, he wonders why they have not beaten him again. Opening one eye to take a peek, he sees his two captors simply sitting there finishing their beers and staring at him as if they are simply making sure that he does not make a run for it.

Being cautious, he wonders what is going on. Don't get him wrong, he is ascetic that they have stopped, but he is wondering why.

Are these two clowns just the first phase? Are they bringing in weapons or other torturing devices? Oh, he so hopes that is not the case. He really doesn't think he can take any more of it. Or, have they actually stopped because they realize that he has nothing to tell them?

He certainly hopes so. If he is lucky, perhaps he can go home soon, but he does not dare to ask. But, of course, it's the not knowing that really kills him. As Max starts to sweat from anticipation, he hears a loud crashing sound as the door bursts open. There are a dozen men in ski masks and rifles.

"Oh, no!" Max laments again.

He is sure he is done for. These people do not look friendly. As he begins to accept his impending doom, he has no idea what else is happening in the building.

Everything is happening so fast, but seems to be in slow motion at the same time. As soon as they blast their way in, there is a stream of shooting as Max cringes behind his

190

armchair with his hands covering over his head, hoping not to get hit.

Even though his hands cannot possibly save him from a bullet if one of the masked men decide to aim at him, it's a natural reflex that a man has when faced with imminent danger. All it really does is make him look like the biggest coward in the world, but that is the least of his worries right now.

Before he knows it, his captors are dead on the ground with a pool of their own blood lying to the shattered beer bottles.

Then, one of the man shouts, "Max, are you OK? Are you hit?"

Still somewhat deaf from the shooting frenzy, Max has no idea who is shouting at him.

All he knows is to nod and say, "I am OK! I am OK!"

Then, the man grabs a hold of his shoulder and drags him out of the building and into a black vehicle as the speed away. Only then does the man pull off his mask. Seeing his rescuer's face puts a smile on Max's face. It's Thom. He has never been so glad to see his friend.

*

It seems that phone call has indeed saved Max's life. After getting the phone call, Thom immediately knew that something was wrong. Ironically, it's because the call was so muffled that Thom became alarmed because there are only two reasons for a jumbled call in this day and age. The most obvious reason is when a person jams the signal so they cannot be tracked by satellites or any other tracking devices such as a GPS or a phone. By bouncing from tower to tower, the signal from the phone cannot be traced. The

191

downside is bad sound quality when it bounces. A second reason is if someone else is intercepting the conversation from a different location, which causes the signals to overlap with each other, causing a muffled effect.

Regardless of which reason it is, Thom knows that the caller is desperate and that time is running out. Thankfully, Max never hung up the phone when he hears his captors return. Instead, the phone got muffled by the cushion seat, so they couldn't hear Thom's voice.

Before dropping the phone, Max could hear Thom faintly say, "Hello? Hello? Are you still there?"

After the captors return, Thom can hear them muttering something. Even though he has no idea what has been said, he can tell from the circumstances that it was definitely a distress call. Based on what he could hear and the panic in the voice, he was certain that someone was in trouble.

He immediately tried to contact Max. When he didn't pick up the house phone, Thom immediately sprung to action. Even if it wasn't Max, and it more than likely was, someone was still in trouble.

Immediately, he went to work to try to figure out the original location of the signal. With one of the most sophisticated signal trackers in the world at his disposal at the Desiderios headquarter, Thom was able to trace it even though the signal bounced from one continent to another.

*

Patting Max on the back, Thom says, "It's good to see you, old buddy. It's been a long time!"

Cracking a smile through a swollen lip, Max says, "Not as good as it is to see *you!*"

"Want to tell me what happened?" Thom asks sympathetically as he hands Max a bottle of water.

Considering that this man has pulled all the stops to rescue him, Max figures the least he can do is give him an explanation. Not holding back on any detail, he recounts how Pete had approached him about his relationship with his father Philip, his analysis of Trip's drink, his meeting with Pete in the coffee shop, and his eventual capture.

"How did you end up in that particular taxi?" Thom asks at the end of the narration.

"I don't know. I just hailed one like anyone would."

"That means they must have been scoping you."

"Maybe, but anyone who has been tailing me should know that I normally take the bus. How would they know that I would change my mode of transportation today?"

"Hm, good point. Maybe the taxi is merely Plan B and they have something else planned for your regular bus."

"That is possible," Max says still not believing what has just happened to him. Then, he suddenly says, "Who were they? Do you know?"

"No, but I have taken their bodies so we can investigate further when we have more time."

"By the way, I don't think I have thanked you yet. From the bottom of my heart, I am so grateful to have you as my best friend. Thank you *so* much for saving my life. I owe you big time, but what else is new?" Max says with a crooked smile.

Smiling, Thom cheerfully says, "Hey, what are friends for, right?"

It's like the old times. Thom is always there to rescue him whenever there is any sign of trouble. Being the bookworm, Max had his share of bullies who taunted him in

193

school, but Thom always took care of it and anyone who had faced Thom's wrath always learned their lesson and never came back to mess with him again. Before long, people started teasing him for being Thom's pet. Although he dreaded those comments, he never told Thom to butt out and mind his own business because he knew that Thom was only doing what he thought was best to protect his friend. Today, he is very glad that Thom continues to be there for him.

*

As they get back to the Desiderio headquarter, Thom takes Max to see Violet immediately.

"Ah, a successful extraction. Good job, Thom!" Violet says.

"I will let Max tell you what happened. I am going to find out who those hooligans who captured him were," Thom says as he takes his leave.

"Were? I see you took care of them permanently. Was it necessary?" Violet asks.

"They were armed and dangerous. Just look at his face."

Nodding sympathetically, Violet takes out a first-aid kit from the cabinet and says, "Anything broken?"

"No, I don't think so," Max replies.

As Violet begins to dress his wounds, he tells her exactly what he had told Thom.

"Wow, all that just for Trip's lunch?" Violet asks as she shakes her head.

"But, it's more than just lunch," Max protests.

"How so?"

"I found an element in the potion that has never been documented before that glows," Max replies as he reaches into his shirt pocket to extract the flower petal. "I think it came from this flower, which is from his hometown Algoma."

"Really? That is interesting. So, what of it?" Violet replies nonchalantly.

"Aren't you curious what it is?"

"No, not really. I see the man drink that thing every day. It is just a nutritious concoction that keeps him strong and alert."

"Hm, still. I would like to analyze the properties of this flower. Even if it has nothing to do with anything, it is a very rare find, and a valuable contribution to the scientific community."

Laughing, Violet says, "Knock yourself out! It's just a flower, for crying out loud."

"Do you know what it is?"

"I have seen it before. I think we have some growing in our garden."

"What is it called?"

"I am really not sure. There are so many different flowers growing there. I don't know the names of half of them. Trip is the better one to tell you. The garden is his baby. You might want to ask him."

Being a little intimidated by Trip, Max says, "No, that won't be necessary, but I would love to take a look at his garden some time."

"Well, like I said, it's his baby. If you want to see it, you will need to ask him first. As far as I know, I am the only one allowed in there, and that's only because he needs someone to take care of them when he is not around," Violet says casually.

Getting the hint, Max drops it.

"There, does that feel better?" Violet asks after stitching up some of the open wounds and putting iodine and ointments on the bruises.

"Thank you, Violet. Who would have thought the Warrior is also Florence Nightingale?" Max says with a smile.

As Max gets up, Thom walks back in and says, "Leaving so soon?"

"Yeah, it's late. I need to get back home."

"Considering what you have been through, do you need a little security detail?"

"Thanks, Thom! You spoil me, but I am going to be fine," Max replies with a deeper voice than usual.

Laughing, Thom knows what he is trying to do, but still says, "Come on, I will go with you."

Since he puts it that way, Max cannot exactly say no. Besides, there is something about the way he said it that is a little odd. He has seen that look before. It's a look of concern, but not simply for safety reasons. He must have found something out and wants to talk to him about it in private.

"Thanks, old friend," Max replies as he heads out the door with Thom.

As Thom gets in the driver's seat, Max says, "Well, what did you find out."

"Ah, ever so observant. That's what makes you such a great scientist!" Thom says.

"Yeah, yeah, you are always such a charmer. So, what's going on?"

196

"Well, as we expected, those two are hired help. They are notorious for kidnapping people for ransom, but they only do it when there is a contract out. They never do it for themselves."

"So, who hired them?"

"We don't know yet. Since they are both dead, we cannot exactly ask them. It's too bad, really. When we charged in, we were expecting to meet a much more menacing force."

Disappointed, Max looks out the window. He is glad to see that at least they are still heading in the right direction.

"What I want to talk about is this Pete that you mentioned."

"What about him?"

"Is there anything else you can think of that can help me find him?"

Confused, Max says, "Isn't he staying at the hotel?"

"He checked out right after you met with him," Thom replies.

Alarmed, Max says, "I don't really know him very well. I have no idea where else he can be if he is not at the hotel. Why do you ask?"

"I have a feeling he is not who he says he is. It's just too convenient of a story."

"But he was talking to my Dad's grave like he was telling the truth."

"Did he say anything that only he and your Dad would know?"

"No, but he is so genuine when he spoke to the headstone."

"Have you considered that maybe he is just a very good actor? Con artists often are."

Looking grim, Max agrees, all the while wondering when Thom became such a cynic. When growing up, he had always been the happy go-lucky kind of guy. It's too bad really. The Thom he knew was so much fun.

"Do you have anyone you think may want to kidnap you?" Thom changes the subject.

Max blushes at the question because his first thought was Thom and his second was his mother Amelia. He is too embarrassed to tell him the truth. How can he? He knows he would freak out if someone accuses *his* mother of wrongdoing, if she were alive, no matter if it's warranted or not.

Instead, he just says, "No."

Knowing his friend too well, Thom teases, "Oh, come on! You are so totally lying! Who is it? You most certainly have someone in mind. Tell me!"

"No, I don't," Max denies it even though his eyes betray him before the words come out of his mouth.

"Man, I thought we tell each other everything. Why are you hiding this from me, especially after all that I have done for you? Didn't you just thank me for saving your life not very long ago?" Thom continues to clown around with him.

"OK, but you have to promise you will not get mad first," Max says, knowing full well that it is a mistake.

Once he goes down that road, he is not going to be able to retract it. Meanwhile, Thom knows that he is not going to like what Max has to say. Every time his friend says those words, it usually means:

"Brace yourself for what you are about to hear because it's going to be bad."

Nevertheless, it just makes Thom wants to know the answer that much more.

Instinctively, he replies, "I promise."

After taking a deep breath, Max says, "Your mother."

"What?" Thom shouts in disbelief as he is visibly disturbed by Max's reply.

"You promised!" Max protests.

Clearing this throat, Thom blurts out, "I am not mad! What makes you think I am mad?"

Max looks at him in silence.

After taking a few deep breathes, Thom's breathing is starting to slow down a little. Even though his mother has been angry with him since Victor's downfall, he still loves her very much. Even if she probably does not believe it, he would do anything for her.

When he has cooled down enough, he calmly says, "Can you tell me why?"

Max says, "Are you sure you want to hear it?"

The question is meant to give Thom a moment to ask himself if he *really* wants to hear it, but it just makes Thom a little more anxious than he already is.

"Yes, I am sure!" Thom says.

Not wanting to make his friend any more fretful, Max gives him a rundown of his earlier analysis of the small building in the woods where he was held captive, paying special attention of the immaculate Greek busts and the exquisite design of the chair cushion.

"Really? You think my mother is behind your kidnapping because the building is decorated? You are kidding me, right?" Thom replies as he laughs.

"I am sorry, but she is the only one I can think of who would bother to decorate an interrogation room like that?"

"What are you saying? That my mother is a woman of excesses?"

"Come on, Thom. Please don't be like that. I am just telling you what I think. I may be completely wrong."

"Soooo wrong!" Thom affirms.

"I am sorry that I have upset you. That's why I didn't want to tell you."

"Well, I am glad you did. Now I know that you don't trust my mother."

"That's not what I am saying! That's not what I am saying at all!"

For the rest of the trip, neither man said another word to one another until they approached the Sullivan Estate.

"Look, I am really sorry, OK? Please don't be mad at me?" Max begs.

"I am not," Thom replies unconvincingly.

"Do you want to come in?"

"No, that's all right."

With that, Thom drives off, leaving Max feeling like dirt.

Chapter 15: The Confrontation

Knowing that Thom is still very upset, Max is worried that his friend is going to get into an accident. There would be no way he can forgive himself if something bad would happen to his best friend. After having survived so many battles together, he is not about to let his friend get hurt, or worse, die like that.

Instead of heading into the house, Max decides to get into his car instead. If he had done that this morning, none of this would have happened and he wouldn't still have the throbbing pain all over his body.

For once, he is glad that he lives in such a remote area. Out here, there are only so many roads that one can take and only one that Thom must take to get back into town. Hence, even though it has already been over five minutes since Thom left, Max knows he can still catch up to him if he drives a little faster. He is hoping that Thom is not peeling off the road at too fast of a speed. It is dark and there are no street lights in this part of the road. There simply are not enough cars to justify the expense, which makes it that much more dangerous for Thom to be driving out of there angry and preoccupied.

Soon, Max sees the headlights of a car in front of him. He is sure that is Thom. It's late and the old folks who live out here are usually in bed by this time. Before he can reach the vehicle, however, he turns off to another road. Puzzled, Max wonders if he is following the wrong car. Because he does not see any other car, even at the speed he has been going, he figures that it must be Thom. As he drives on the new road, he gets an eerie feeling in his gut as if he has been here before. With no road signs, he has no way of knowing for sure, but the last time that he was on a road with no road signs, he was a prisoner in a taxi.

The thought is less than comforting. Instead of trying to make sure that his friend gets home safely, Max is starting to wonder if that is his friend at all. Taking a cautious approach, he slows down and leaves a longer distance between him and the vehicle in front of him. He is starting to regret his decision to take that turn. If that is not Thom, he is hoping that the driver is not a bad person. What if this is an associate of one of his, now deceased, captors? As Max continues to let his imagination run wild, he sees brake lights up in the front.

"Oh, no," Max mutters to himself.

Has the driver finally noticed that he has been following him? Is he going to get out of the car and get into an altercation? Worse, is he going to be kidnapped again? Slowing down, he makes sure that all of his windows are closed and the doors are all locked. Then, the car in front of him turns again left into what looks like bushes.

Although one part of him screams, "Stop and turn back!" another part of him wants to see where this will take him. He figures as long as he has control of his car, he can just speed off if there is trouble ahead. Besides, except for the moon light, it's completely dark out here. If he turns off his headlights and hide, they may not be able to pursue him, but he is hoping that it will not come to that.

"That sounds like a good idea," Max says to himself as he turns off the headlights before making the same turn.

As expected, the bushes are only there to disguise an entrance. Once he gets closer, he sees a large locked iron gate with a security booth just on the inside with no one inside. From there, he sees that the car he has been following is already parked inside the property and the driver has already exited the vehicle. Looking at the large property, Max wonders if this estate belongs to Amelia Richardson. Even though he and Thom were close as children, he had only been to their main house. He has never seen their country home before, if you can call this massive thing that. It is about the same size as the main house, but looks more like a chateau.

He feels safer now that he thinks Thom has merely gone to see his mother. At the same time, if Amelia was the one responsible for his kidnapping, is Thom going to be in danger if he tries to confront her? What else can he be doing at his mother's house at an hour like this? Is she capable of hurting her son? No, that is not the same woman he knew as a child. No matter how angry she may be with him, in her heart, she will always love him.

On the other hand, if Thom accuses her of wrongdoing, what will she do? She is not going to just take it at face value. In all probability, she is most likely going to try to sway him and turn him to her cause. After all, Thom is vulnerable right now. He cannot bear to have any more guilt from her. A part of him must want to redeem himself in her eyes. It's entirely possible that she can sway him to do something that he would not do normally. There is only one way to find out.

Stopping his car right outside of the bushes, he tries to hide it from the road and the chateau. He is pretty sure that there are cameras everywhere to detect intruders. After surveying the area, he finds a section of the wall that is partially obscured by the tree branches. In the dark, it should be virtually impossible for the security camera to pick up.

"Here goes nothing," Max mutters to himself as he tries to scale over the wall.

Now that he finds a potential entry point, he has to figure out how to get up on it. Once again, it's a lot harder than it looks in movies, where they simply jump up, grab the top, and hoist themselves over, ever so effortlessly. There are no trees or other tall structures where he can simply use to jump from one location to another, like some of the crazy stunts you see on television. Being well over 15 feet in height, the wall is designed to prevent such attempts. Even if he can do it, he doubts he has the muscle strength to do it in one step. He needs to be able to scale it some other way. He tries several different methods.

First, he tries to take a running start. All that accomplishes is it gives him about an extra foot or two up the wall before falling back down. He is still nowhere near the top. Then, he tries to put his fingers and the tips of his feet into the cracks between the bricks to try to climb up. This method is extremely tiring, but seems to be somewhat effective – at least for the first few steps.

After the first couple of steps, he is starting to feel like he is getting the hang of it, literally, as he hangs on the wall like an insect. As he is about to congratulate himself, however, his foot gives out and he falls back down, just a foot shy of the top. Having twisted his left ankle on this last attempt, Max is not about to try that again. If he does manage to break his foot, he is going to be in deep trouble as no one will be there to save him. Sitting against the wall for a minute, he wonders what else he can do.

Looking at his car, he thinks to himself, "Of course, why haven't I thought of that earlier?"

Putting his car in neutral, he pushes it under the bushes and wedges it as close to the wall as he can. Stepping over the hood to the top of the car, he can easily jump up to reach the top. Putting all of his energy into his arms, he tries to hoist himself over. With the help of his feet, he can feel his arms quiver a little before he is able to get to the top. Once he is on top, he faces another challenge – the way back down.

Even though he has never admitted it to any one, he is faced with the painful reminder that he is afraid of heights. Instead of standing up on the wall, he simply crouches on top of it. As his body wobbles a little, he makes sure that his hands never leave the wall, not even for a second. Then, shifting his body to face the other side of the wall, he lowers his body down, all the while gripping to the top. It is not until he finally gets back on the ground on the other side does he realize that his hand is bloodied from the climb.

There is nothing much he can do for it right now. Keeping off of the lights, he runs towards the main house as quietly as he can. Trying every window, he finally finds one that is open on the second floor. Even though there is a tree right outside of the window for him to climb up, he is not looking forward to it since his hands are still swollen from his previous adventure. Nevertheless, he does not see any other option. Mustering all of the courage he has, he scales the tree and into the open window.

His heart is now pounding faster than ever before, even during the Six Year War. As a sharpshooter, he needs to focus. Being a good distance away from the enemy, he has always been calm. It's different now. He is standing in the middle of someone else's home. This is definitely new territory for him. For the first time in his life, he is the *bad guy*. It's exciting but scary at the same time. He is hoping that he is indeed in Amelia's house. He would hate to be trespassing in someone else's home. If he gets shot, the owner can always claim self-defense. He *really* hopes it will not come to that.

*

As he looks around the room, he sees exquisite pieces of artwork. Although he does not see any Greek sculptures or fine art from famous painters from the Renaissance, there is no doubt that the owner of this owner has the same taste as the one who decorated his little interrogation cell. He is looking for something that will tell him definitively who really owns this place before he starts to explore, a picture, an envelope, a writing sample, anything personal. If he can determine that he is in the wrong place, he can still sneak back out as if this never happened. Unfortunately, this looks like a simple guest room.

Max can smell the freshly laundered sheets. That can explain why the window is open. After the previous guest departed, the owner is probably cleaning out the room, including the air. Snickering quietly, Max wonders if the guest has bad body odor or something similar to require such treatment. Then, a macabre thought comes to him. What if the reason for the ventilation is because the previous guest has died in that room? Ewww! The thought gives him goose bumps everywhere.

Finding nothing of use in this room, Max decides to take his chance. As soon as he opens the door to venture out, he can hear muffled voices coming from below. Tiptoeing towards the sound, he can tell that it is indeed Thom and his mother talking with one another in the living room. Taking a small sigh of relief, he figures at least he is not going to be shot by a random stranger. Peeking out from the top floor, he can see that mother and son are both sitting on the couch, both sipping from a glass. Thom looks visibly calmer than when he was driving him towards his house earlier. It has been over an hour. Who knows? That glass of wine probably helped.

"Why are you doing this?" Max hears Thom asking.

"There is no need for you to worry, darling. Everything is fine! You are overreacting. It's really not that big of a deal," Amelia reassures him.

"How can you say that? He is my friend!" Thom rebukes.

Hearing these three lines, Max is concerned. What are they talking about? What does Amelia plan on doing? Is *he* the friend that Thom is arguing about? Of course, Thom does have *other* friends. Max is not conceited enough to think that he is the only one.

In this case, he is hoping that it is *another* friend. He certainly does not want to get in the middle of whatever it is that they are arguing about. One thing is for sure. Thom doesn't look very happy, but that doesn't seem to be bothering Amelia. From the look on her face, she looks determined to continue her plan regardless of what her son says. At least, it doesn't look like she is going to hurt Thom in anyway. So, it doesn't look like she is a complete monster even if she may be a kidnapper.

"Is he really? What has he done for you lately? Besides, all you need to know is that this is way bigger than one man. I am trying to save an entire country of people and right what was wronged. You know me. It's no different from any of my other charitable projects. In time, I am sure you will understand," Amelia continues.

At first, Max is infuriated by that sentence.

"How can she possibly say that I haven't done anything for Thom lately?" Max thinks to himself.

Even though it is true that Thom comes to his aid more than he does for him, it is only because Thom does not need any saving! He visits his friend as often as he can when he is in town, but lately, Thom has been keeping to himself and refuses to open up as much as he used to, which puts a cramp in their friendship, but that, in no way, means that they are not there for one another!

After his initial anger simmers down, however, he replays the conversation back in his head and quickly realizes that they may in fact not be talking about him. At first, he thought the conversation is about his kidnapping, but now he is not so sure. What country are they talking about? As far as Max knows, neither Thom nor Amelia has ever been outside of Balavan, which just shows how little he really knows about his best friend. Hence, not knowing that Amelia is the benefactor of the Algomians, he has no a clue as to what county they are referring to.

"No, I will not. I cannot just sit by and do nothing while you toy with people's lives," Thom replies.

"Come on, darling. Give your mother a little credit. I am not playing with people's lives. I am saving them. There is a huge difference!" Amelia argues.

It's interesting that the words coming out of Thom's mouth does not seem to support his action. For a man who seems to be so determined to stop his mother, his body language is certainly very tame. Is he so exhausted after a full day of rescuing him that his body no longer has the zest to put up a fight? Or, does he really believe his mother and is only arguing against her because of principle? Or, another possibility is that he may be saying it for someone else's benefit. Is someone else listening in? Curious, Max quietly walks across the hallway to take a peek inside the other rooms. He is so thankful that the floor is made of marble. If it was made of wood, he would certainly have made an awful squeaking sound, considering how quiet the rest of the house is.

As he looks from room to room, many of them are closed. He does not dare to try to open them in case there are people in there. From what he remembers, the Richardsons have a good number of servants, including several gardeners, cooks, maids, chauffeurs, security guard, and butler. Any of them could be sleeping in any of these rooms. It is already 2AM, which is past bed time for most people, including the hired help.

If he remembers correctly, however, every time Amelia is up, there is usually one servant who is up with her in case she needs help with something. It's strange that none seems to be around. It's as if she made sure that no one is up to listen to her conversation.

Then, under the door of one of the rooms, Max can see light. He knows there is someone is still awake inside that room, but is afraid to find out whom. He figures it's not worth the risk of being discovered.

He or she is probably just minding his or her own business. Yet, if Amelia does not want any witnesses, why is this person awake? It does seem somewhat odd. As he continues to check the rooms, he can hear some light snoring. Before long, he figures out that all of the rooms that are occupied are closed and there is no point checking any of the room that is open. The only suspicious room is the one with the lights on.

Going to an empty room two door down, he hides in it. It's the perfect place to continue listening to the conversation downstairs and to monitor the lit room. Sitting in the corner to avoid all light, he wonders what has he gotten himself into and how does he plan on getting out of it if he gets caught. No matter what, he is already knee deep in it. There is no point regretting his decision to intrude on the Richardsons. As Thom and Amelia's conversation continues exactly the same way he has since Max started eavesdropping, he still has no clue what exactly they are talking about.

He starts to get comfortable on the plush carpet and stares at the closed door. Unfortunately, he picked a place that was too comfortable and at the end dozes off in the room after a while.

Chapter 16: Death of a Matriarch

Suddenly, Max is woken up by a loud sound. Not sure what is going on, he jumps up abruptly. Then, he hears gunfire followed by footsteps running and sounds of screaming. Panicking, Max looks down and sees that Thom is holding on to his mother, rocking her with tears coming from his eyes. Even though he has blood all over him, it looks like Amelia's blood. Even from up there, he can tell that she is dead, as blood continues to flow out of her.

There is a gaping hole in the wall that was blown wide open just seconds before the shooting started. Forgetting that he is trespassing, Max runs down the stairs to his friend. From the corner of his eyes, he can see hired help peeking through the cracks of their doors, too afraid to come out and investigate. Although they all obviously heard the chaos down there, they are all hiding in their rooms. Some are crying while others are whimpering.

"Are you alright, Thom?" Max shouts.

Not even looking up, Thom just mumbles, "Why? Why?"

Max has never seen his friend so vulnerable before. It's not like him to not be running after the attacker. The Thom he knows certainly would. But, something seems to have snapped in this proud man. After losing Victor, his adoptive father, Thom was depressed, but never shed a tear, at least not in public.

After losing Fouke, his biological father, Thom was angry for not knowing him until it was too late. Now, Thom is completely distraught over the death of Amelia, his adoptive mother.

Despite his complaints about her and the recent events that have driven a humongous wedge between them, she is the only mother he has ever really known and is the only one he truly loves.

Sensing that Thom is too frozen to leave his mother, Max has to step up and do something before the perpetrator gets away. He immediately runs towards the hole and looks outside. He sees a large black truck with something big and bulky in the bed covered with a black tarp peeling off the driveway. It looks like there is some sort of a military grade gun in the back. The front gate has already been blown open on their way in. Even though his instinct is to go after them, he knows that he is not going to be able to catch up to them.

Running to the security booth, he is hoping that the system has captured footage of the truck even though it is unmanned. Considering that Amelia had no reason to be on high alert, he is hoping that she has not turned off the recording features, especially at night when all seems to be quiet. There are so many buttons in the booth that he is having trouble finding the switches to even see if he can find any useful footage. After a few trial and errors, however, he finds the recording of the truck approaching. Looking inside the front of the cab, he sees two men wearing the same ski masks as his captors.

After his captor's death, have their associates come back to Amelia for revenge? Why would they? It wasn't Amelia who killed them, unless, of course, they blame her for leaking the plan and compromising their mission. Continuing viewing the tapes, he gets a license plate number and scribbles them down, hoping that it will lead them to the murderers even though he knows very well that a professional hit man would use fake plates even when they are in the dark.

They must know that a chateau as big as this one must have some form of security detail. Considering that the guard has already gone home for the day and there is not a replacement for the third shift, however, it does seem woefully inadequate. Perhaps, the murderers know about this. If so, they must also know that the security booth contains footage. If they do, he needs to save the recordings before they come back for it. With the recording and tag number in hand, Max runs back to the main house.

Thom has not moved since he last saw him. Picking up the phone, Max calls the police. Within the hour, the house is filled with investigators and reporters. The scene is even more chaotic now than when the incident occurred. The hired help have finally emerged from their rooms.

None of them saw it happen. No one bothered to question why Max was there. Being Thom's friend, they simply assume that he had gone there with him. Meanwhile, Thom is too distraught to talk to anyone. He simply has a glazed look over him. It took paramedics a great effort to pry his dead mother off of his arms.

It's as if *he* has a dead grip on her. When the investigators finally leave, Max finally tries to talk to his friend again.

Offering him a glass of water, Max says, "Can you hear me, Thom?"

Thom nods without lifting up his head up. Max puts the glass down on the table in front of his friend before taking out the disk with the recording of the killers.

"The attackers look like the same people who kidnapped me. It's all in here," Max says in a solemn voice.

With those words, Thom's eyes widen as they meet Max's. It seems those words have brought Thom back from his trance.

"Let me see!" Thom says as he grabs it and puts it in the computer.

As he views it, he looks very determined and angry, but does not say a word.

"Do you recognize them?" Max asks.

Thom shakes his head without taking his eyes off of the screen as if he is memorizing the image of his mother's murderers, even though he can only see their eyes and mouths.

"Do you have any idea why they would want to target your mother?" Max asks, being careful not to use the word kill.

Again, Thom shakes his head.

After a short pause, Max says, "Please let me know if you want me to shut up, but do you think this has to do with my kidnapping?"

Turning towards Max, Thom says, "It's possible, but she wasn't the one who hired those men."

Surprised, Max says, "How do you know?"

Thom simply looks at him. While he knows that his friend does not mean any harm by his words, they still hurt.

"I am sorry. I don't mean to falsely accuse her of anything. I just want to know if there is a reason why you know for sure. Maybe we can use that information to catch the perpetrator," Max tries to explain.

"Because she told me," Thom simply replies.

So, it would seem that Thom did confront his mother about the kidnapping and she denied any involvement in it. Max has never known Amelia to lie to her own son, except for his own birth, of course, but that is because of a promise made to the birth mother. What if she lied here, too, to protect someone else? It's definitely a possibility, but he is not about to go down that road right now, considering how fragile Thom's psyche is right now.

Nodding, Max says, "I am going to talk to the staff to see if they saw anything."

Thom nods.

Max heard some of the staff members talk to the police. None of them seems to know anything, but they may not have asked the right questions. Going upstairs, he can tell that some of them are still visibly shaken. Then, he passes by the room that he remembers seeing with the lights on earlier. It is now empty and clean. It seems whoever was there carefully cleaned up before leaving. Since he does not remember seeing anyone leave the room before the murder, it seems very suspicious to him. Whoever it was may have something to do with the murder. Looking into the next room, the door is half open and a woman is simply sitting on her bed.

Knocking on the door, he says, "Excuse me. I'm Max. I am wondering if I can ask you a question."

The frightened young woman quietly whispers, "Sure."

"Are you alright?" Max asks.

Nodding, the woman seems to imply that she is, but she obviously does not seem to be.

"Can I get you anything? Some water or blanket?"

Nodding, she says, "Water would be nice. Thank you."

Returning with a glass of water, he says, "Do you know who was staying in the room on your left?"

Nodding, the woman says, "Yes."

"Where did that person go?"

Surprised at the question, she blinds blankly and says, "I have no idea."

"Is it one of the workers?"

Shaking her head, she says, "No, it's one of Mrs. Richardson's friends."

"Do you know who it is?"

"I think his name is Pete."

The sound of his name sends a shock wave into Max's gut. Can it be? Can this be the same Pete who has been trying so hard to be his friend? The same one who is trying to get him to analyze Trip's drink? Who is he?

"Does he come by often?" Max continues his questioning.

"Not too often. He comes by every month or so."

"How long ago did he starting coming around?"

"I am not sure. It must have been years."

Max is surprised that he has never seen or known of this Pete before if he has been coming by for so long.

"What was his business with Mrs. Richardson?"

"I don't really know. They always speak in private."

"Does he always stay in that room?"

"As far as I know, yes."

Their need for privacy seems to indicate that Pete and Amelia might have had a romantic relationship, but because they always stay in separate rooms, however, that may not be the case. With Victor out of the picture, there should be no reason why they have to meet in secret if it's not a personal relationship.

If that is the case, what is Amelia doing with this man? And, why do they have to maintain their secrecy? And, more importantly, why has he disappeared? Did he know about the attack ahead of time? Worse, was he the one who instigated the attack? The thought is almost too horrible for Max to imagine.

"Thank you for your help," Max says to her. She nods at him and sips at her water.

Max gets up and leaves the room before returning to Thom.

"Did you know Pete before I told you about him earlier today?" Max asks his friend.

"No, why do you ask?"

"He has been coming to visit your mother regularly for years."

"What are you saying?" Thom replies with a disgusted look on his face.

"Oh, no, I don't think it's like that," Max says knowing that Thom probably assumes the same thing that he did at first.

"Then, what is it?"

After Max tells his friend what the maid told him earlier, Thom becomes livid.

"That bastard!" Thom screams as he storms out of the house.

"Wait! Where are you going?"

"Where do you think? To find that bastard who killed my mother!"

"How do you plan on finding him?" Max asks.

By then, Thom has already left. There is no point trying to follow him this time. By the time Max has reached his car, Thom is already out of sight. There is no stopping him this time. Going back inside Amelia's home, Max ponders what he should do. It isn't until now when everything has quieted down does he realizes how tired he is. His eyes just couldn't stay open. He sits down on the couch and before he knows it, he has fallen asleep.

*

At dawn, the sun is rising coming up on the horizon through the gaping hole in the wall, which shines into Max's face. Twitching, Max awakens in a panic.

"Oh, no!" Max mutters.

He does not remember falling asleep. He is hoping that Thom has not done anything stupid and gotten himself killed.

Jumping into his car, he speeds his way to the Desiderios headquarter and tells Violet everything that happened the night before.

"Why didn't you tell me earlier?" Violet says in frustration.

Max knows that precious time has gone. The assailant is now long gone and the trail is already cold.

Trying to defend himself, he says, "At least the police are already working on this case."

"You are going to trust the life of your hands in their hands? They are only interested in solving the murder case. They are not even looking for Thom, let alone trying to save him," Violet says.

"Where do you think he has gone?" Max asks sheepishly.

Looking at her watch, Violet says, "He has been gone for, what, three hours?"

"Yes, that's about right."

"Trip left about two hours ago."

"Oh, no. You think the two of them are hunting this Pete down?"

"I believe so. They packed heavy."

Violet knows Trip well enough to know that this is very unusual. Trip is a very careful but also strategic man. He never packs so much heat unless he is almost certain that he is going to face enemy fire. For the common thugs, a simple piece or knife is all he needs. There is no point scaring off the prey prematurely by displaying the weapons. He also never takes off with just one man like that unless it's urgent, especially in the middle of the night like that. Thom must have been very convincing, which is very worrisome.

"Where do you think they went?" Max asks.

"I can only think of one place – Algoma," Violet replies.

There is only one reason why these two would team up together on their own – a common formidable enemy who is about to be out of their grasps if they do not hurry. Although they are both brilliant fighters, they have very different tactics, which can damper each other's efforts. While Thom prefers an all-out war to end everything quickly, Trip prefers to go after the primary target to prevent too much unnecessary bloodshed. At the same time, Thom is trying to catch his mother's killer while Trip is trying to prevent the destruction of his hometown.

"Should we go after them?"

"No, I have a bad feeling about this," Violet says with a very serious tone.

Max has never heard her sound so grim before. She is supposed to be the happy one in the group. Even during the Six Year War, Violet has always kept an upbeat attitude. She knows that during a time like that, someone has to in order to keep up the morale. For her not to go after Trip means that she thinks it's important for her to stay here and there is only one reason for that – she is expecting something *really* bad to happen in Balavan.

"We all do," Max replies rhetorically.

What he doesn't realize is that Violet is not just talking about the murder or Thom's mission for revenge. It's much bigger than that. No one goes out of their way to attack a matriarch like Amelia Richardson like that. Everything about it stinks – the timing, the method, and the people involved. It's all planned and professional.

"What do you think is going on? So many things have happened in the last 24-hours. It's quite unsettling," Max continues.

Nodding, Violet is pretty sure that it's a preemptive strike of some kind, but she doesn't want to tell Max her suspicious just quite yet. After Trip's departure, she already beefed up the security around Balavan without alarming the citizens. She always believes in being overly prepared rather than under prepared. She knows that as soon as Amelia's death is announced to the public, there will be many speculations around the streets. If she doesn't keep her suspicion under wraps, it can become paranoia.

Trying to get as much detail as possible, Violet says, "I know you probably rather put it all behind you, but I really need you to tell me everything you remember about your kidnapping and what you saw, heard, felt, or believed when you were in Amelia's chateau. It's important that you don't leave out any details."

Over the next half hour, Max goes through everything he can think of as Violet takes mental notes of every word that comes out of his mouth.

"So, do the decorations from the kidnapping site match any of the ones you found in Amelia's home?"

Thinking really hard, Max shakes his head and says, "No, I don't think so."

"So, it's safe to say that it is all a setup," Violet concludes.

"Setup for what?"

"To make Amelia look like the bad guy. You said it yourself. You thought she was behind your kidnapping."

"Then, why kill her?"

"That's a good point. Whoever set her up and killed her obviously knows her well. So much so that they knew exactly where Amelia is sitting when she was having a conversation with her son in her own home. That is the only explanation as to why Thom was not shot when they blew open the wall and gunned her down."

"What are you saying?"

"I think there is a mole in Amelia's household."

"One of the servants?"

"It's likely, but I think it's your new friend Pete. Like you said, he disappeared right after the murder occurred. Did you see a car speeding off besides the men who actually pulled the trigger?"

Shaking his head, Max says, "But it was very chaotic. I could have missed it over the loud sound of screaming."

"In either case, he ran right afterwards. Why would he do that? Where can he go in the middle of the night?"

"So, what are you saying? Pete is the one who set up Amelia and is the mole for told the shooters where to find her?"

"Yes."

That is quite an accusation. Just hours ago, Pete has tried so hard to gain his trust. For a brief moment, he thought he has found someone who knew and cared for his father, but now, it seems like everything is a lie.

"So, why do you think Pete was so interested in finding out what was in Trip's bottle?" Max asks.

"He isn't. It's just an excuse to get you involved."

Max has never felt so betrayed.

"Why?" Max has to ask.

"Think about it? Why would Trip leave something of value in a trash can knowing full well that someone may be snooping around? Did Pete give you a valid reason for analyzing it? I am pretty sure he gave you *a* reason, but do you really think what he told you made sense?"

Max simply looks at the ground.

"I know it sounds harsh, but I believe he recruited you as bait."

As if betrayal is not enough, Violet has added another reason for Max to feel like mud – being used. He feels so dirty that he wants to take a shower right now.

"Knowing that you know Amelia has exquisite taste, he made your holding cell look like something she would do. If you think about it, it's really kind of ridiculous. Why would anyone put valuable art work in a holding cell? Have you asked yourself that question? The only reason I can think of is to lead you to make false assumptions, which seems to have worked out perfectly," Violet explains.

"I still don't understand why he would kill her, though," Max asks as he shakes his head.

"All I have are only theories. I believe Pete did not get the desired result after framing Amelia for the kidnapping. Perhaps, he had wanted Thom to betray his mother and kill her instead. Or, maybe he is hoping that you would take your accusation to the police so they can freeze her assets. There are many possibilities, but none of them happened. Amelia still had her fortune and Thom still loved his mother. Hence, he has to resort to plan B."

221

"But he didn't give enough time for those things to happen."

"Maybe Pete is a very impatient man."

"I don't think he is. He seemed awfully patient when he was trying to convince me of his friendship with my Dad."

"OK, maybe he wanted to kill Amelia to begin with, but decides to destroy her reputation first."

"That is a possibility, but why would Pete do something like that? From what I heard from the maid, he seems to be a longtime friend."

"Maybe she betrayed him and he is looking for revenge."

"Like what? It is quite an elaborate scheme just to humiliate her first."

"Or, maybe he is not the master mind, but just the mole pulling the strings."

"Then, who do you think is the really behind it all?"

"I don't know, but I think Trip does. Whoever it is, I am sure he is dangerous."

Chapter 17: The Secret Unfolds

As Violet fortifies Balavan, Trip and Thom are hot on the Pete's trail. Riding in their custom designed motorcycles, it's nearly impossible for Pete to spot them at the distance they are keeping.

It's super quiet and fast and has a special stealth cover makes them look nearly invisible when they are moving, which is definitely a good thing. Even if Pete is not aware that they are following him, he would be scared just by their appearances.

With war paint on their faces, they look downright intimidating. Although they have already spotted him, they do not want to confront him. From what they already know about him, he is not likely going to be able to tell them anything useful. Short of a good torturing session, it's also not likely that he is going to yield anything new or even truthful.

Instead, they are pretty sure he is not the master mind behind it all. Staying a good distance away, he wants Pete to take them to the *real* culprit behind the scenes. By the time Pete is in sight of Algoma, however, he veers off to the right onto a dirt road. Putting his goggles on, Trip sees a building about a mile down the road that is carved into a rock formation.

Maybe, a building is not the right word. It looks more like a bunker, which is certainly consistent with the rest of the Algomian architecture. Once Pete reaches the bunker, he waits there patiently for the gate to open. Being a heavy door, it takes some time for it to rise completely, giving Trip and Thom just enough time to get there. Before Pete knows it, the two motorcyclists have zipped by Pete's car and into the bunker.

Being in stealth mode, however, they have kept their identities hidden so far. In fact, Pete has no idea what just happened. All he knows is that there is a sudden gust of wind on both sides of his car that seems to go into the bunker. Suspicious, he gets out of his car to investigate. He can see tire tracks, but discounts them as old tracks that must have been left behind. After all, many other people also have a fondness for motorcycles.

From Pete's nonchalant expression, it seems whoever he is meeting is probably one of them. Besides, his eyes were firmly on the gate in front of him. There were no motorcycles or any two wheeled vehicles that could have possibly gone by just now. Instead, staring up into the sky, he wonders if there is a storm coming and that it was just a miniature cyclone that is common in those parts. Looking around to make sure that he is alone, he gets back in his car, drives into the bunker and closes it as if it is just any other garage in a home.

Stopping just inside the door, Pete gets out. Just like in Algoma, he picks up his hand and a well camouflaged door opens in the bunker wall. Being as quietly as possible, Thom and Trip both tiptoe behind him, mimicking every single move.

It would almost look comical if a third party is watching, but it has to be done. Knowing their security system, they have no other way of getting inside the lair without being detected. Just as quietly as they followed him in, they both get up into the ceiling panel of the elevator and hide in there by the time the door opens. As expected, they hear a voice. Unlike the elevators that Trip has seen in Algoma, this one does not close itself, which allows the two stowaways to get a good view of what is happening below.

"Welcome home, Pete," a man's voice says as he gives Pete a hug.

224

From the top of the elevator, Trip can tell who he is meeting. As expected, it's Drew, but it's a different Drew. Unlike the mean and sarcastic one that he met in Algoma, this one is friendly and cheerful. He is full of smiles.

"Thanks, my friend," Pete says with a big grin.

"So, did everything go as planned?" Drew asks.

"Oh, you should have seen it! It's perfect! Amelia did not see it coming! You should have seen Thom's expression, too. It's priceless! That bastard was so distraught, rocking on the floor like a helpless little child. I don't think he'll think straight for months, let alone stop us!"

Seething with anger, Thom cannot believe Pete seriously underestimates him like that. On top of that, he is making fun of him for mourning the death of his mother. What kind of monster does that? It takes every bit of his energy not to jump down and kill him with his bare hands. He knows it would be premature. When the time comes, he will be sure to really let him have it before killing him. At least now there is a theory why they kidnapped Max. It seems they know about Max and Thom's relationship and have predicted that Thom would confront his mother. They want him to witness the death of Amelia in order to destroy his mind. Well, it didn't work.

"I am glad we finally got rid of that annoying benefactor. It's long overdue. We haven't needed her for so long," Drew says with a smug look on his face.

"Benefactor? So, after all of this time, it is Amelia who saved the Algomian children?" Trip thinks to himself.

He is having a difficult time wrapping that around his mind. After what Victor has done to them, how in the world is that possible? But then again, he now understands why Thom is the way he is. Both he and his mother have been trying to make amends for what Victor has done and they both have suffered for it. Thom may never be himself again, but at least he didn't have to pay with the ultimate price like his mother did.

By his side, Thom has a confused expression on his face. It's obvious that he heard the same thing from Drew's mouth, but unlike Trip who has a little more insight on what is going on, he does not know much about the new Algoma. Being a man of little words, Trip never bothered to tell him before they left. Being in a hurry to capture his mother's killer, Thom never bothered to ask anything. Hence, he has no real clue what the benefactor has done, let along any history between her and Pete besides what Max has told him. But, now, he has starting to get the picture and his level of disgust towards the two men below is increasing by the second.

"Yes, you can say that again. That bossy witch always has to have the last word," Pete agrees.

Why in the world would Drew and Pete want to kill her after all that she has done for them? And, those adjectives are simply awful. What in the world could she have done to be called a bossy witch? Yes, she can be a little bossy at times. Somebody has to, especially when she is surrounded by a bunch of children. And yes, she can be mean; too, if you get on her wrong side, but not any more than many people you meet on the street. After all the sacrifices that she has made for them, it's definitely uncalled for. It seems like they are discarding her once they have become self-sufficient and no longer needs her. It is the ultimate betrayal.

"Well, there is only one thing standing in the way of our revenge," Drew says.

"What is that?" Pete replies curiously.

"You," Drew says with a smile before taking out a gun and shooting Pete in the heart.

226

"Why?" Pete cries out as he grabs his chest and falls down.

"You are just as annoying as she was," Drew says as he leans over him.

"But, but… I have always treated you like a son," Pete says in a gasping voice as tears come down his face.

Shocked at what he is witnessing, Thom doesn't know how he should feel. While he is certainly still angry at Pete, he definitely has not seen this coming. It seems Pete is indeed just a puppet controlled by the man he thought loved him as a son. If he wasn't blinded by Drew, he may not have done any of the awful things he did and his mother would have been alive.

"You are just a useless and lame excuse for a man! I cannot believe how much effort I have to put into you for you to do what I wanted!" Drew says, adding insult to injury.

At least Trip is convinced that this is the real Drew. That means the nice, smiling one is nothing but a show. Then, a thought comes to him. Does that mean that he is acting when he is around his family, too? If he is, Simone and her children are in danger, and he cannot let him hurt them. But, is she in on it? Trip doesn't know anymore.

"With you two out of the way, I can launch that attack that I wanted to launch before that demon Victor died. No more listening to you babbling about what I should do. Like you have a clue! You are nothing without me!" Drew continues as he smirks and spits on his face.

By then, Pete has already lost too much blood to be able to hear him. His body stills as his head falls to the side. Even Trip is starting to feel bad for Pete. Although he has never liked Drew, he never thought he is capable of being so harsh and cold to another human being. Worse, he cannot believe that Simone has married this monster.

227

Does she know the real him? If she does, is she a two-faced jackal, too? He cannot allow himself to think badly of her, but he cannot shake the possibility. After all, a woman always knows her man, even if she does not want to admit it. Just the thought of her having to live with him gives him the creeps. In his book, he is no different from Victor. While the methods are totally different, they are both heartless creatures that do not care about anyone else besides themselves and does not care who they have to hurt or kill in order to get what they want.

*

"Come on out, you two," Drew says as he looks up in the elevator and smirks.

Both Trip and Thom are surprised that he knows they are there. Is that a part of his plan, too, to draw the two of them out there? It doesn't matter. If Drew thinks he can take two of the strongest leaders in this part of the world, he has another thing coming. He will have to be either the most delusional man on earth or the most confident. Either case, Trip and Thom are ready for him. Opening the ceiling tile, the two men calmly jump down to the elevator floor below, both with rifles in hand pointed at Drew.

"Hello, Drew," Trip says.

"This must be the famous Thom I have heard so much about," Drew replies while looking Thom up and down in disgust.

Snapping his fingers, all four of Drew's clones come out from behind a fake wall and start shooting.

Thom and Trip both turn to edges of the elevator to avoid the bullets, only going out in the open to shoot at them.

228

"Cover me," Trip says to Thom as he nods.

Trip runs out of the elevator, ducking as low as he can before grabbing the man on the far right and slashing at his arm with the knife. He cries out and drops his gun as Trip elbows him in the stomach. He takes him and slices his neck to the bone to finish him off.

He holds out his body in front of him as a shield and runs toward the next man. He dropped the dead body and tackled the man before wrestling away his gun from him. He goes to shoot him, but before he can, one of the others aims his gun at Trip.

Trip ducks but hisses as he feels a bullet penetrate his left shoulder. He looked up at the man and shoots him multiple times, twice in the head and once in the chest.

While he was occupied with the shooter, though, the man he'd wrestled to the ground shot up and grabbed his handgun from its holster.

Trip looked back at him just in time to see him start to pull the trigger. Before he can, though, a hole opens up in his chest, with a stream of blood spattering his uniform.

The man coughs up blood and falls back down before going still.

Trip looked behind him and nodded at Thom, who was still holding his own gun up. Thom nodded back before turning his attention on the fourth man, who'd been hiding behind a pile of crates to avoid the bullets Thom had been shooting at him.

The man peeked out and saw that all of his comrades had fallen. His face was frightened, and if he'd run right then, there would've been no doubt that Trip would have let him leave without any inhibitions.

Unfortunately, this man was Liam, the father of Simone's sweet little niece Tiffany, and he would do anything to protect Algoma.

He ran out, shouting and shooting bullets at Thom with his machine gun. Thom hit the floor, covering his head, but the barrage stopped almost as soon as it had started.

He moved his arms away from his face and saw that it was Trip who'd stopped him with a bullet to the head.

Thom started to get up, but he felt a sharp pain in his right calf when he attempted to stand.

"Aggh!" He leaned against the wall, putting all of his weight on his unhurt leg. He could see the blood welling up already, soaking his pant leg with red.

He grimaced but there was no time to do anything about it. Drew was still there.

He looked up at the carnage and sighed. It'd only taken a couple of minutes to end the life of four men.

The same three people are still standing, Drew, Trip, and Thom. While Trip and Thom are both bloodied and breathing hard, each with bullet wounds, Drew is completely calm and unscathed as he walks out towards them.

"Worthless," Drew says as he looks at his dead comrades on the ground.

It seems the coward has been hiding when his men were shooting. Yet, he had nothing but insult for them.

Seeing the laser from Thom's scope on his head, Drew smirks again and says, "Go ahead. Shoot an unarmed man. That would be fitting of a bastard like you."

He held his arms out like an invitation, not expecting him to actually do anything. Unfortunately, Drew certainly knows how to push people's buttons. Without a second thought, Thom pulls the trigger, putting a bullet into his head.

Drew stills with a look of shock apparent on his frozen face.

As Drew falls down, Thom says, "About time he shut up!"

While Trip does not approve of him shooting an unarmed man, he has no problem making an exception for this one.

"What now?" Thom asks, thinking that he has avenged his mother with the demise of Pete and Drew.

Before Trip can utter a reply, however, Drew gets up. Shocked, Thom and Trip both point their guns at him again.

"How? How is it possible?" Thom screams in disbelief.

With an assault rifle like that, he knows the damage that it can make. With the right angle, he has split many men's skulls in half with them. Yet, there he is. He can clearly see the bullet hole in Drew's head and the blood that is coming out of it, but it doesn't look very deep. In fact, he does not see any brain matter exposed at all. Strangely, it looks more like a flesh wound than anything else, but Thom knows that he had a good clean shot. How is it possible that he is still alive? Worse, how is he able to get up?

"That hurts, you bastard! I cannot believe you actually shot me!" Drew says as he rubs his head.

Thom simply stares at Trip in disbelief with his mouth open. Trip, on the other hands, does not look troubled at all. In fact, it now finally makes sense to him. He knows exactly what is going on. Drew has found the secret – the same one that Trip has harbored for nearly two decades.

The difference is that Drew has increased his dosage by roughly tenfold. If that is the case, it is bad – very, very bad, not just for Trip and Thom, but for Drew as well. While it would make Drew virtually indestructible, it also has a very deadly side effect.

It goes far back to the days that he would rather forget – Victor and his men's vicious attack on his beloved Algoma. Starving and delirious, young Trip did not know if he was going to live or die. At a time like this, a boy's body shuts off as many unnecessary bodily functions as possible in order to stay alive.

With only his survival instincts intact, he knew that he had to eat something in order to survive. Despite not knowing whether or not something was poisonous, he gathered as many types of wild vegetation and insects along the way as he could, eating only when he must. Not knowing how long he may have to live on these meager meals on the road, he ate sparingly. Eventually, his little body collapsed along the road.

When he finally woke up in Violet's family caravan, he realized that he still had two pockets full of beautiful wild specimens. Being a nature enthusiast, he replanted as many of them as he could. By the time they settled in Balavan, he had transferred them into his beloved garden and continue to tend them till this day. As he grew older, he began to study them and crossed pollinate them to create new breeds. It was solely for educational purposes. Eventually, he discovered that the right combination of them produces a flower that can help strengthen every part of his body, from his organs to his skin. It has a distinctly bright yellow glow to it, just like the flower petal that Max has found.

Although he was very excited about his discovery, he soon figured out that too much of it started to give him headaches. Then, he started to have paranoid thoughts. Before long, he learned that the new plant that he has created has distinct side effects that slowly deteriorate his brain functions if taken in too high of a concentration.

232

After a series of trial and error, he has figured out the perfect combination for his formula. Mixing it with other nutritious ingredients like eggs and leafy vegetables, he began to drink it regularly. Eventually, it becomes the only thing he consumes.

He has kept his formula a secret because of a fear of abuse. After all, once people figure out that he is essentially wearing a human armor, one of two things may happen.

First, people may try to test him by trying to shoot him or hurt him in some way, just to see how far he can go. Second, people may try to take too much of the potion, thinking that it may make them indestructible, without thinking of the consequences. That is exactly what Drew has done.

Drew has become so addicted to the formula that he has thrown all caution to the wind. Judging from his behavior, he believes Drew only has very few months to live if he continues his current dosage.

"Surprised? I know all about you and your little secret, Trip," Drew continues in a cocky voice.

"What is he talking about?" Thom asks.

"El Diablo," Drew mutters as he spits on the ground. "What a joke! I am much stronger than you are!" Drew says in a taunting voice.

"Ever since I heard about your prowess, I have been studying you. I knew there is something odd about you. So, I stole a bottle of your precious potion and had it analyzed. I just cannot believe you opt for such a weak version of it when you could have so much more! You must be a bigger loser than I thought! What's the matter? Cannot handle it?" Drew continues with laughter.

Looking at Pete's dead body, he says, "How do you suppose it ended up in the trash of your rental home? That stupid Pete actually thought you left it there. What an idiot! I cannot believe that he thinks someone as careful as you would leave something that important in the trash! Well, at least I was able to use it to my advantage. And, here is the fruit of my labor! You, the famous El Diablo standing right there in front of me for me to annihilate! With you out of the picture, I will be the most powerful and feared man in the world!" Drew exclaims.

Trip looks at him with a cold and emotionless expression. Thom knows that look. It means he is ready for anything. As Drew lounges for him with his bare hands, Trip drops his rifle and decides to hone in on his martial art skills instead. Apparently, both men know that there is no point shooting at one another. While it will definitely hurt quite a bit, neither one of them can be killed by a bullet.

As Drew starts to swing at Trip, it's pretty obvious that Drew is not nearly as gifted in hand-to-hand combat as he thinks he is. In fact, he may not be gifted in anything at all. He hid behind the wall during the earlier gunfight. He was also conveniently absent during the kidnapping or the murder. There is no evidence that he can even defend himself.

Based on this match, it seems the only talent he has is to be a punching bag. At least, it looks like he can take a hit. On the other hand, Trip is not making it easy on him. He delivers one punch after another without stopping, with exact precision. If he was a common man, Drew would have passed out by now, but with so much of the potion in him, he doesn't realize how close to death he really is.

Knowing that Trip is an honorable man, Thom knows he would not want him to interfere with the fight. Instead of just standing guard, however, he decides to check out the rest of the bunker. Since this is unchartered territory for him, there is no telling if there are other hidden dangers lurking in the dark. From what he has seen so far, Thom is

234

pretty sure that nothing is beneath Drew. When he finally realizes that there is no way he can win against Trip, Drew will probably take out some sort of secret weapon to blindside Trip and take him out. Thom needs to find it before that happens.

As Thom surveys the room behind the wall, however, he is jerked back by Trip shouting "No!"

As he imagines the worst, Thom's heart nearly stops.

"Is it possible? Did Drew actually defeat Trip? No, it cannot be, can it?" he thinks to himself frantically.

As he bursts open the door, he is not thinking of his own safety or welfare as he takes out a long sword ready to stab Drew with it with as much force as he possibly can. Before him, he sees Drew's body on the ground, convulsing uncontrollably, with blood and foam coming out of his mouth.

"What happened?" Thom exclaims.

Standing back up, Trip says, "There is nothing more we can do for him."

Finally recognizing that he cannot possibly win against Trip in his current condition, Drew did the unthinkable. He took a concentrated dose of his potion, which is already a dangerous dose as it is. As soon as he drank the first sip, he dropped to the floor and went into a seizure. Within a minute, Drew stops shaking.

"What happened? Why did you scream?" Thom asks.

"I was trying to stop him from killing himself."

"Why? I thought you wanted him dead."

Shrugging his shoulders, Trips replies, "I guess it was a reflex."

The truth of the matter is he does not want Simone to be a widow. No matter what kind of a monster Drew was, she and her children do not deserve to suffer for his mistakes.

*

With Drew and his clones' deaths, Simone becomes the one and only de facto leader of Algoma. As Trip delivers the news to her, she looks solemn, but does not look surprised.

"How are you holding up?" Trip asks.

"OK," she replies.

With a pleading eye, she continues, "But we need a new leader, one who can fix Drew's mistakes and make Algoma great again."

"That's what you are."

"No, a real leader," Simone says with a sad smile.

"Thanks, but I already have a home," Trip replies.

Looking sad, she says, "I understand, but if you change your mind, I will always be here with open arms."

Epilogue

Taking up her new role in full force, Simone has decided to redo a lot of things in Algoma, starting with the security system. While still keeping the surveillance in some of the key places like the entrance to town, she has removed all of the ones that may invade one's privacy. She has also starting building actual bridges so visitors can come in without fearing for their lives. In the future, she plans on moving the town back up to the surface, like real human beings again. And of course, she has thrown out any plan to launch a war against anyone, least of all Balavan, a dominion that has never done them any harm. In time, Algoma may return to its former beauty. Who knows? Maybe one day, Trip will find his way back there permanently.

When Drew was alive, she never cared for them, but also never spoke out against him or his ideas. The truth is she misses him a great deal. Before he started taking the potion, he did love her more than the world and did everything he could to make her happy, even when he knew that her heart is not always there.

With each passing day, he became to become more and more distant from her, but even then, he continued to be an excellent father to her children. Hence, she never allowed herself to see how far off the deep end he was. It is a mistake that she will have to live with for the rest of her life.

To preserve his memory, however, no one besides Simone, Trip, and Thom really knows the truth behind Drew's death, especially his children. Officially, he died from a tragic heart attack when he was on a surveying mission.

As for Thom, he is learning to live with the loss of his mother Amelia, but it's a difficult journey. Not ready to say goodbye to her yet, he has kept all of her possessions as well as some of her staff. On the nights that he comes over to her chateau, he is often heard talking to her, asking her for forgiveness and for her guidance. He is also known to tell her about his days and how much he misses her. It seems he has fallen off the deep end, talking to a ghost, but he doesn't care.

News of Thom's strange behavior reaches Victor's ears in his solitary cell. When Victor hears that his beloved Amelia has died, he is inconsolable. That very night, he tries to hang himself with anything he can tie together. As soon as the suicidal thought comes to Victor, however, Thom gets a very vivid dream from his mother, telling him to go to the headquarters. Without directly telling him what is going on, she tells him exactly where to go before he wakes up abruptly. Jetting out of the house immediately, he follows her directions exactly. Just as Victor is about to put his neck on the noose, Thom arrives at his cell.

With his eyes wide open in shock, he shouts, "Stop!"

Surprised, Victor looks at his son. It seems so long ago when he last saw him. He almost didn't recognize him.

"Why?" a much deflated Victor asks in a weak voice. "What else should I live for now that the love of my life is dead?"

"Because she told me to stop you from killing yourself."

At first, Victor thinks Thom is lying to him, pretending that Amelia is not dead, but after looking deep into his eyes, he knows what he means.

"I am sorry for what I did to you," Thom says sincerely.

With those short words, tears come to Victor's eyes. It seems the old man has forgiven him, too. In a strange way, he is closer to both Victor and Amelia now than ever before. He also seems to have made peace with them. Perhaps, in time, he may become his old self again, too.

And Trip? Trip was the same as always, laying on his hammock, swaying gently in the breeze, his garden beautiful as ever.

About the Author

Megan H. Lee is a college student in North Carolina. She started writing books in elementary school and has kept her passion for literature. The idea of the Balavan series started when she was in middle school, and years in the making have contributed to make the book. This is her third novel written in collaboration with her mother Sylvia S. Lee, who adds to the intrigue and suspense of the series with her love of history and imagination.